NODDY™

STORY BOOK
TREASURY

NODDY™

STORY BOOK
TREASURY

Enid Blyton

Collins

An imprint of HarperCollinsPublishers

A letter from Noddy

Hallo, girls and boys!

I'm your friend Noddy! When I nod my head, the bell on my hat goes 'jingle-jingle', and everyone knows it's me.

I live in a little house called "House-for-One" which I built myself! It's got a garage for my little yellow car, which I use for driving my Toyland friends wherever they want to go. They have to pay me sixpence, though!

I've got lots of friends in Toyland – the Tubby Bears, Bumpy-Dog, Mr Plod the policeman and many more. My very best friend is dear old Big-Ears. He lives in a Toadstool House in the woods. In this book you can read about some of our adventures. I'm sure you will enjoy them as much as we did!

I've promised to take Mrs Tubby Bear to the shops, so goodbye for now!

Love from

Noddy

CONTENTS

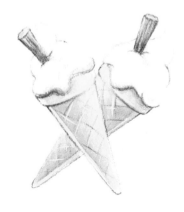

CONTENTS

CONTENTS

CONTENTS

STORY BOOK
TREASURY

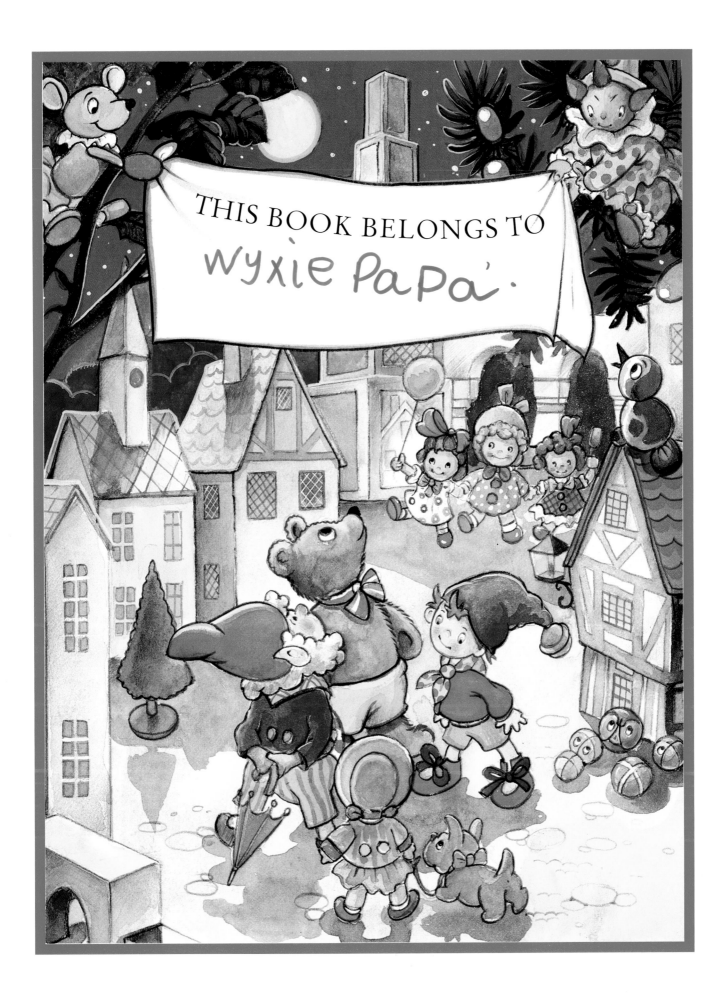

THIS BOOK BELONGS TO

Wyxie Papa'.

Big-Ears and the
Naughty Trick

Big-Ears was busy washing his bicycle. He had a big sponge and a bowl of soapy water. His bicycle was going to be sparkling when he had finished!

"Mmm, it's certainly very clean," Big-Ears said to himself thoughtfully when at last all the washing was done. "But it's not very shiny. I'll pop into my house and see if I have any bicycle polish left."

The moment Big-Ears had gone, two figures appeared from behind the trees. It was the goblins! They crept towards Big-Ears' bicycle to play a mean trick on him. Big-Ears was in his house for quite a while.

He searched every cupboard for some bicycle polish. But there was not a trace to be found! "Oh, why didn't I remember to buy some polish when I went to Toy Town this morning?" Big-Ears tutted crossly as he stepped out of his house again. "I can be so forgetful sometimes. I'll just have to ride all the way to Toy Town again!"

But just as Big-Ears was about to climb onto his bicycle, he spotted a large round tin in the basket. It was a tin of bicycle polish! "Now where did that suddenly come from?" he asked himself, mystified. He stroked his beard. "It must have been there all the time," he said, starting to CHUCKLE. "I must have bought some polish this morning, after all!" Big-Ears chuckled again and again, as he started to polish his bicycle.

"I must be getting even more forgetful than I thought!" he grinned. Big-Ears polished and polished until his bicycle gleamed like a new pin.

"Perfect!" he smiled. "I've never seen my bicycle looking so shiny. I'm so proud of it, I think I'll just go for a little ride before putting it away!"

So Big-Ears climbed on to his bicycle.

"Just a very short ride," he promised himself. "And a very careful one, too. I don't want to ride my bicycle into any puddles or I'll have to wash and polish it all over again!"

As soon as Big-Ears started to pedal, though, he rode right into a puddle.

He had wanted to go *forwards* but his bicycle had gone *backwards* instead.

"That's strange," Big-Ears said to himself. "I'm sure I was pedalling the right way. Now, let me try again."

This time Big-Ears was even *more* careful, but again exactly the same thing happened. His bicycle went *backwards!* "Perhaps I'm on a bit of a slope and my bicycle keeps running downhill," Big-Ears said with a frown. "I'll try pedalling much faster this time."

SPLASH! SQUELCH

Big-Ears pedalled as hard as he possibly could, and suddenly his bicycle went WHOOSH!

"Oh dear! Oh deary me!" Big-Ears cried, as his bicycle sped backwards, weaving between the trees. "Help, someone! HELP!"

Suddenly Big-Ears turned his head and saw a large dip in the ground.

"Oh no!" he cried.

BUMP! BUMPITY BUMP!

"Goodness, now I'm sore!"

But something even more dangerous was approaching from behind. It was Noddy's car!

"Move to one side, Big-Ears!" Noddy shouted. "You're in the middle of the road. And why are you going *backwards*?"

Big-Ears clapped his hands over his ears as he heard a frantic

PARP! PARP! PARP! from Noddy's car. But there was nothing he could do. His bicycle would not stop speeding backwards.

"Look out!" Noddy cried. "You're going to hit my car!"

Fortunately, Noddy managed to steer his car out of the way just in time.

Big-Ears' problems were far from over, however. His bicycle kept going, bumping over the ground, until finally it rolled down the river bank.

"What's wrong with your bicycle all of a sudden?" Noddy asked, as he helped pull Big-Ears out of the river. "It seems to have gone mad!"

"Yes, it does, doesn't it?" Big-Ears said very crossly. "And I think I've just worked out why. You see, I found a tin of polish in my basket. But it was no ordinary polish. It made my bicycle go the wrong way!"

"Well, who could have put it in your basket?" asked Noddy.

"It must have been the goblins," said Big-Ears.

"Oh, of course!" exclaimed Noddy. "Who else would play such a naughty trick?"

Big-Ears suddenly shivered. He was longing to get back to his Toadstool House so he could dry himself by a nice cosy fire. But first he had a job to do.

"Can I give you a lift home, Big-Ears?" asked Noddy.

"No, thank you, Noddy," he said, climbing onto his bicycle. "I have worked out that if I pedal backwards, I will go forwards."

But when Big-Ears started to pedal backwards, the bicycle also went backwards. Again, he ended up in the river!

"The water must have washed the goblins' polish off," Noddy said, as he helped pull Big-Ears out of the river again. "Try pedalling forwards this time."

This is exactly what Big-Ears did and, sure enough, the bicycle went forwards. "Hurrah!" cheered Noddy. "Will you be going straight back home now?"

"Not quite yet," replied Big-Ears. "First, I'm going to pay the goblins a visit. And to get my own back on them, I'm going to pretend that my bicycle is still out of control. So they had better WATCH THEIR TOES!" he said, with a hearty chuckle.

MR SPARKS

TO THE RESCUE

It was a very exciting day for Mr Sparks. He had a new car-wash at the garage.

"I'll just check that everything works," he said to himself proudly. He turned on the tap. He could hear a nice **gurgle, gurgle** inside the hose. Then he went to the other end of the hose. "That's funny," he said, as he lifted the hose. "Where is the water?"

But at that very moment the water started to gush out, SQUIRTING him in the face.

"Ah, it works perfectly!" Mr Sparks said with delight. "All I need now are some customers!"

It was not very long before Mr Sparks heard a PARP, PARP coming in his direction.

"Ah," he said to himself with a smile. "That must be Noddy's car!"

Mr Sparks was hoping that Noddy's car would not be very clean. He was in luck. As the little car came into view, Mr Sparks saw that it was not quite as shiny as usual.

"Hello, Noddy!" Mr Sparks called. "Would you like to try my brand new car-washing service? It will make your car nice and clean again."

"Will it?" Noddy asked eagerly. "I've been so busy giving people rides this morning that I haven't had time to clean it myself."

"It will only take five minutes,"

Mr Sparks said. "Just jump out of your car and I'll switch on my special hose."

So Noddy switched off his engine while Mr Sparks went into the garage to turn on the tap. But just then, it started to rain *very* heavily!

"I won't be needing your car-wash after all, Mr Sparks," Noddy called. "My car will get clean in the rain!" And at that, Noddy turned on his engine.

"But, Noddy!" Mr Sparks called after him as he came out of the garage. "NODDY!"

He was too late, though. Noddy and his car were gone.

"Well, I can't blame him," Mr Sparks muttered to himself. "Who wants a car-wash in the rain? I'll just have to hope that the rain soon stops."

But the rain did not stop. It just became heavier and heavier.

Poor Mr Sparks. His new car-wash was not going to be busy today!

"Perhaps I'll have more luck with my breakdown truck," Mr Sparks said to himself. "I'll drive it around Toy Town and see if anyone needs help."

But Mr Sparks was not lucky with his breakdown truck either.

He drove it all the way to the harbour and all the way back again but he did not meet one car. Where was everyone?

"I suppose no one wants to go out in heavy rain like this," he grumbled. "What a miserable day I'm having!"

Mr Sparks was not the only one who was having a miserable day. Noddy was, too. He suddenly appeared at Mr Sparks' garage. And he was *very* wet and *very* cross.

"Mr Sparks, you must help me," he said. "After I left you, I drove to Big-Ears' house to see if I could borrow an umbrella."

"Very wise with all the rain, Noddy," Mr Sparks said. Then he lifted his hat to scratch his head. "But where is the umbrella, Noddy? You're as wet as a fish!"

"I never reached Big-Ears' house," Noddy explained. "The rain had made it so muddy in the Dark Wood that my car got stuck. I need your breakdown truck to pull it out!"

Mr Sparks was delighted to be able to help. "Just wait here, Noddy. I'll fetch the truck."

Soon they were ready to set off. "Don't worry, Noddy, we'll be at the Dark Wood in a flash!" said Mr Sparks.

And in a flash they were. Noddy's car looked such a sorry sight stuck in the mud. The mud came halfway up the tyres!

"Never mind, Noddy," said Mr Sparks. "My truck will soon pull your car out." Mr Sparks pressed a special button in his truck so that the big hook at the back started to come down.

When it was low enough, Mr Sparks attached it to Noddy's car. Mr Sparks then sat in his truck and started the engine. He made the engine go a bit faster, then a bit faster. At first nothing happened. But then it started to move forward very slowly. And Noddy's car started to move as well!

"Oh, thank you, Mr Sparks, thank you!" Noddy cried. "My car isn't stuck any more!"

Mr Sparks was also delighted. He loved using his breakdown truck. And this was not the only business he would be doing today. Noddy's car now needed a very good clean and this time there was no rain to do the job.

"It looks as if you'll have to use my new car-wash after all, Noddy!" Mr Sparks chuckled.

Mr Plod and
the Stolen Bicycle

It was a very dull day in Toyland.

"I do wish something exciting would happen," grumbled Mr Plod.

Around the corner rushed Big-Ears, puffing and panting. He bumped right into the policeman.

"Assaulting an officer of the law, are we?" asked Mr Plod crossly.

"You must help me!" Big-Ears gasped. "My bicycle was stolen as I was picking mushrooms in the woods."

"That is a serious crime indeed," said Mr Plod. "I must investigate at once!"

The policeman went to the place where mushrooms grew. It was the darkest, most frightening part of the woods. As he walked through the trees, the leaves beneath his feet CRUNCHED and the twigs CRACKLED.

"It is an offence for an officer of the law to be frightened," Mr Plod told himself sternly. He whistled loudly to make himself feel brave. Suddenly the policeman heard a rustling sound. Nervously he shone his torch high into the trees. Two blackbirds were building their nest. He crouched down and peered beneath some bushes. A family of rabbits scampered out of sight.

"AHH!" Mr Plod nearly jumped out of his skin as a squirrel ran over his foot. "I should arrest you for frightening a police officer!" he shouted angrily.

Then Mr Plod tripped and fell to the ground.

THUD!

"What on earth...?" he cried, getting up.

He had fallen over a mushroom basket. Big-Ears must have dropped it when the thief stole his bicycle!

"A clue!" said Mr Plod excitedly. But where was Big-Ears' bicycle now?

The policeman bent down. There on the ground was a tyre track which led deeper into the woods.

"Aha! The thief must have taken Big-Ears' bicycle this way," said Mr Plod, and he crept quietly along, following the track.

A stream trickled through the woods. But Mr Plod was following the track so carefully that he didn't notice the stream at all.

Until...

He was up to his knees in water! "Oh, bother!" he exclaimed. By now Mr Plod was very wet, very cold and very cross.

He climbed soggily out of the stream and saw in front of him a shabby little hut. The tyre track led right to its door!

Wanting to be as quiet as possible, Mr Plod got down on all fours and crawled slowly towards the hut. When he reached it, he peeped nervously in through the open door. Something hit him right in the face!

"STOP, IN THE NAME OF THE LAW!" Mr Plod shouted. But it was only a pigeon flying out of the hut.

Mr Plod looked round, and there in the corner was Big-Ears' bicycle. There was no sign of the thief.

"I've had quite enough excitement for one day!" Mr Plod sighed,

climbing onto the bicycle. "And at least
I *have* recovered stolen property!"
He began to cycle slowly back
towards Toy Town.

Mr Plod was almost home when
he heard a familiar PARP! PARP!

"That's young Noddy's car," he said.
Sure enough, as he cycled around
the corner, he saw Noddy's car in
the middle of the road.

"Causing an obstruction, are we?"
Mr Plod asked sternly.

"Oh, Mr Plod, thank goodness you're here," Noddy cried. "My little
car has stopped and I need someone strong like you to give me a
push."

"Jump in and I'll soon have you moving again," said Mr Plod, climbing from the bicycle.

He leaned forward and pushed the car with all his might. It did not move. He turned round and pushed it with his bottom. It still did not move. He sat down on the bumper wondering what to do next. The car zoomed away and Mr Plod fell to the ground.

"That's all the thanks I get!" grumbled the policeman. He picked himself up and climbed wearily back onto Big-Ears' bicycle.

As he approached Toy Town, Mr Plod could hear a brass band playing.

"I go out for one day," he moaned, "and I come back to find a disturbance of the peace! Someone will be arrested for this!"

But as he turned the corner, Mr Plod opened his mouth wide in astonishment. He rubbed his eyes in amazement. Then he began to roar with laughter.

High across the street was a huge banner which read:

**YOU'RE THE BEST POLICEMAN
IN THE WORLD, MR PLOD!**

Standing beneath it were all his Toy Town friends.

"But, Big-Ears," said Mr Plod nervously, "I didn't find the thief who stole your bicycle!"

"Oh, but there wasn't one!" laughed his friend. "We all wanted to thank you for making Toy Town such a safe place to live. I pretended that my bicycle had been stolen so that we could surprise you with this party!"

"Wasting police time is a serious offence," said Mr Plod. "But I am prepared to overlook the matter this once!"

Everyone laughed. Even Mr Plod.

The Goblins

and the Ice Cream

It was a hot, lazy afternoon in Toyland. Sly and Gobbo had been asleep all day.

Sly stretched very slowly.

Gobbo yawned very loudly.

And they both rubbed their eyes.

"Come on, Sly," said Gobbo, getting to his feet. "All this sleeping has made me very hungry. Let's go into Toy Town to have an **ICE CREAM.**"

It was a long walk from Goblin Corner into Toy Town. The goblins felt even more hungry when they got there. At the ice cream parlour, they flopped down and ordered two **ENORMOUS** ice creams.

"Delicious!" slurped Sly.

PARP! PARP!

Noddy's little car stopped beside the goblins.

"Hello, Noddy," said Gobbo. "Would you like to join us for an ice cream? You must be very hot driving around Toyland on a day like this."

"That is very kind of you, Gobbo," said Noddy. "An ice cream is just what I need."

Noddy got out of his car and sat at the table with the goblins.

When Noddy's ice cream arrived, Sly and Gobbo gobbled down what was left in their own bowls.

Suddenly, Gobbo pushed over his chair. Sly leapt right over the table and they ran from the ice cream parlour knocking over Mr Wobbly Man on their way.

"I say," said Noddy in surprise. "Where have those wicked goblins gone? Oh no! Now I'm going to have to pay for all THREE ice creams."

Gobbo and Sly ran and hid behind a market stall. They danced and cackled with delight. Gobbo suddenly stopped. "All that running and laughing and dancing has made me very tired," he gasped. "What we need is a ride home."

PARP! PARP!

"That's Noddy!" said Sly. "Do you think he will give us a lift?"

"Yes, if we ask him nicely," laughed Gobbo.

The goblins leapt out in front of Noddy's car.

"Hello, Noddy," said Gobbo. "We're very tired. You will take us to Goblin Corner, won't you?"

"No I will not, you HORRID goblins," said Noddy crossly. "I had to use the money I was saving for some new tyres to pay for your ice creams. If I don't buy some new ones soon, I won't be able to drive my car. And then I won't have any money at all."

"We forgot our money, that's all," said Gobbo. "If you drive us home to Goblin Corner, we'll pay you for our ice creams and give you two sixpences each for the ride!"

"All right," said Noddy slowly. "But you MUST give me the money. And Sly, you will have to sit on the spare wheel at the back of the car."

So off they set in Noddy's car.

When they had almost reached Goblin Corner, Gobbo pointed to something in the dark wood.

"What's that?" he shouted.

Noddy SCREECHED to a halt and turned to look. Gobbo grabbed hold of a tree branch and somersaulted out of the car. Sly leapfrogged from the spare wheel and they both ran into the woods.

"You wicked goblins!" cried Noddy. "Now my tyres are even more worn and I still have no money. I'm going to fetch Mr Plod."

It was turning dark when Sly and Gobbo heard the PARP! PARP! of Noddy's car in the woods. They scrambled up a tree so they would not be seen.

Then they saw Mr Plod get out of the car and saw the light from his torch shine into the bushes.

"Well, young Noddy," said the policeman. "It's too dark to find those villains now. I wonder if they'll be greedy enough to show their faces in Toy Town tomorrow?"

"Why is that?" asked Noddy.

"It's the ice cream eating competition, that's why," replied Mr Plod. "Let's see what happens tomorrow."

Off they drove back to Toy Town.

The next day it was hot again.

"Just the kind of day for an ice cream eating competition," laughed Sly.

"Yes, indeed!" said Gobbo. "We must make sure Mr Plod doesn't see us."

The goblins couldn't believe what they saw when they got to Toy Town. Huge tables were crammed with enormous, colourful ice creams.

Master Tubby Bear was lining up for the competition with Mr Wobbly Man, Mr Sparks and Clockwork Mouse, and all the other toys were cheering.

"Come on, Sly," said Gobbo. "Let's show them how much ice cream WE can eat!"

"Yes, let's!" laughed Sly.

"Not so fast, you villains!" shouted a voice behind them.

It was Mr Plod.

"Quick!" shrieked Gobbo. "RUN!"

Sly did run... straight into Gobbo.

THUD!

They fell into the bowls of ice cream.

SQUELCH!

And the tables **CRASHED**

to the ground.

Gobbo and Sly were covered in

a sticky, gooey mess!

"I knew you couldn't resist all this ice cream,

you wicked goblins!" said Mr Plod sternly. "Now you must pay

Noddy all the money you owe him. AND you must pay for his

new tyres."

Gobbo and Sly sighed. "We promise!" they said.

"You mark my words," said Mr Plod, pointing at the goblins who

were dripping with ice cream. "Villains like you two will always meet

a sticky end!"

Tubby Bear and the
Decorating

Tubby Bear was often naughty. But this morning he was EXTRA naughty.

First, Tubby Bear banged his drum all around the house. It gave poor Mrs Tubby such a headache.

Then Tubby Bear tore up his mother's favourite recipe. He threw all the little pieces into the air to make a snowstorm.

Then, worst of all, Tubby Bear rolled marbles all over the kitchen floor. Mrs Tubby Bear slipped on them and dropped her tea tray.

"I've had ENOUGH for
one morning!" Mrs Tubby Bear
complained to Mr Tubby Bear.
She wiped her hot, furry brow with her apron.

"When you go to decorate Noddy's house, you'll have to take
Master Tubby with you!"

Tubby Bear was delighted that he was going to Noddy's house. "Can
I help you decorate?" he asked excitedly as he walked with his father
along the road. "Can I dip the brushes into the paint? Can I stand on
the ladder? Can I paint the ceiling?"

"No, you may do none of those things!" Mr Tubby Bear told him
firmly. "You would make far too much mess. You are to sit quietly on
a chair in the corner!"

Tubby Bear was very unhappy sitting on the chair at Noddy's house. He frowned as he watched Noddy and his father put up the ladder. He sniffed as he watched them take down the curtains. He wiped away a tear as he watched them open the paint tin. It was Tubby Bear's favourite colour. Bright pink!

"I'm getting a bit bored staring at yellow all day," Noddy explained to Mr Tubby Bear. "So I thought we would paint all the walls a nice pink."

Mr Tubby Bear scratched his head. "But, Noddy," he growled, "you will need more than one tin of paint if you want to paint ALL the walls."

"Will I?" asked Noddy. "In that case, I had better drive my car to the paint shop to buy some more tins. Will you come with me to make sure I buy just the right number?"

Mr Tubby Bear did not know what to do. He thought he should go with Noddy to the paint shop. Noddy could get so mixed up sometimes. But Noddy's car only held two people. That meant leaving young Tubby Bear behind!

"I don't mind," Tubby Bear said from his chair in the corner. He was a lot more cheerful now. "I don't mind being left behind. I promise to stay in my chair!"

Mr Tubby Bear stroked his chin. Could he trust Master Tubby? It was at that moment that Mr Plod the policeman passed the open window. Noddy suddenly had an idea...

"Hello, Mr Plod!" Noddy called. "Are you on your rounds? Could you just peer in next time you pass, to make sure Tubby Bear isn't doing anything he shouldn't?"

"I will indeed," said Mr Plod. Noddy and Mr Tubby Bear felt very happy as they left the house. They were sure Tubby Bear would not do anything naughty NOW.

But as soon as Noddy's car had driven away, Tubby Bear jumped down from his chair. He made straight for the biggest paintbrush and thrust it into the tin of paint.

"I *will* help decorate," he sniggered naughtily. "I will, I will, I will! And one tin of paint is PLENTY for all the walls. As long as I just do spots!"

Tubby Bear started at the wall with the window. He painted great big spots on one side... then on the other side... and then underneath the window.

The naughty bear was really pleased with himself. He thought pink spots looked so smart!

Tubby Bear was just about to paint another wall when he heard whistling outside the window. It was Mr Plod! Tubby Bear hurried back to his chair in the corner.

"Hello, young scamp!" Mr Plod called through the window. He could not see the wall with the pink spots. "Glad to see you are behaving yourself! I'll tell Mr Tubby Bear and Noddy when I see them."

Tubby Bear smiled as Mr Plod went on his way. The naughty bear ran back to the paint tin but – oh dear! – he ran right into the ladder and knocked it over.

Oh dear! again. As Tubby Bear was jumping out of the way of the ladder, he stepped straight into the paint tin. There was hardly any paint left. Not even enough to paint spots! Tubby Bear returned to his chair very miserable indeed. Very messy, too!

This was exactly how Noddy and Mr Tubby Bear found him when they came back from the paint shop.

"Mr Plod was just telling us how good you have been, Tubby Bear..." Noddy began. Then his eyes nearly popped out of his head. "Look at my wall!" he cried. "How will we remove all those spots?"

"And look at your carpet!" Mr Tubby Bear gasped. "And look at YOU, Tubby Bear. What a terrible mess!"

After a while, though, it was decided that things were not too bad. Mr Tubby Bear said they could easily paint over the spots on the wall. Noddy said he was going to throw out the carpet anyway. It was quite old and would not go with pink walls.

That just left Tubby Bear.

"A hard scrub should sort him out," chuckled Mr Tubby Bear, grabbing hold of one of Tubby Bear's ears.

"Yes!" said Noddy as he grabbed the other ear. "A VERY LONG hard scrub!"

Mr Straw's
New Cow

It was a very busy morning on Mr Straw's farm. All the animals had to be fed, the cows had to be milked and the eggs had to be collected. Mrs Straw usually fed the animals, but she wasn't there today. She had gone to look after her sister who was ill.

PARP! PARP! Noddy drove into the farmyard.

"Hello, Noddy my lad, what can I do for you?" asked Mr Straw, rushing out to meet the car.

"Mrs Straw asked me yesterday if I would lend you a hand," explained Noddy. "But I've got TWO hands you can borrow if you want!"

"Well, I could do with some help, Noddy my lad," agreed Mr Straw. "Can you feed the hens?"

"Yes, I can," said Noddy.

When Noddy picked up the sack of corn, the hens **CLUCKED** and scratched around his feet. "Here you are, hens! Breakfast!" laughed Noddy, as he scattered the corn on the ground. His bell jingled as he worked.

"That's a funny hen!" cried Noddy. He turned round. A cow was standing behind him, and she was looking at Noddy with enormous eyes. "Shoo!" shouted Noddy.

"It's all right, Noddy. That's my new cow," said Mr Straw who was walking across the farmyard. "She only wants to be friends. Could you collect the eggs now, please?"

Noddy fetched the basket and placed the eggs in it very carefully. He had just picked up the last one, when there was a loud **MOO!** Noddy was so startled that he dropped the egg. Mr Straw's new cow was right behind Noddy, breathing down his neck.

"You naughty cow," grumbled Noddy. "You frightened me. Shoo! GO AWAY!"

"It looks like she's your best friend now, Noddy my lad!" laughed Mr Straw. "I can manage the rest of the feeding, but could you take six eggs to Mrs Tubby Bear for me?"

Mr Straw gave Noddy the eggs and three sixpences for all his help.

"Thank you, Noddy,"

said Mr Straw. "Don't forget to close the gate as you leave."

Noddy drove out of the farmyard. As he was closing the gate, Mr Straw's new cow began to run towards him.

"Shoo! Go away!" shouted Noddy. He leapt into his car and drove away as fast as he could. Noddy was in such a hurry that he forgot to close the gate. Mr Straw's new cow ran out of the farmyard after her friend.

On the farm it was almost milking time.

"Now, where's that new cow of mine?" Mr Straw asked himself. He looked around the farmyard and saw the open gate.

"I told Noddy to close the gate," grumbled the farmer. "Now my new cow has followed him. Come on, horse. We'll have to find her."

Mr Straw climbed onto his horse and rode out of the farmyard. He made sure that the gate was closed this time, so that all the other animals would be safe.

"I think we'll try Mrs Tubby Bear's house first," Mr Straw said.

"**NEIGH!**" the horse agreed.

What a sight greeted Mr Straw, as he rode up to Mrs Tubby Bear's house! On her washing line was a pair of Mr Tubby Bear's trousers with their legs badly chewed. A muddy pillowcase lay on the grass and a sheet covered in hoof marks was wrapped around a tree.

"This is your cow's fault, Mr Straw," said Mrs Tubby Bear angrily.

"I am sorry," apologised the farmer. "Is the cow still here?"

"Indeed it is not!" replied Mrs Tubby Bear. "Noddy brought in my eggs, and when he left, the cow followed him."

"And where did Noddy go?" asked Mr Straw anxiously.

"He went to see Tessie Bear," replied Mrs Tubby Bear.

"I must go there at once," shouted Mr Straw, and he galloped off through Toy Town.

As Mr Straw's horse **CLIP-CLOPPED** up to Tessie Bear's house, out rushed Bumpy-Dog. **WOOF! WOOF! WOOF!**

"Bumpy-Dog is very excited," sighed Tessie Bear. "One of your cows frightened him in the garden. Then the cow ate all my flowers."

"I am sorry," said Mr Straw. "Is the cow still here?"

"No," replied Tessie Bear. "I think she was waiting for Noddy,

because when he left, the cow followed him."

"And where was Noddy going?" asked Mr Straw anxiously.

"He went to see Big-Ears," replied Tessie Bear.

"Then I must go there too!" shouted Mr Straw, and he galloped off towards Toadstool House.

Noddy's car was outside Big-Ears' house. So was Mr Straw's new cow. She was trying to eat Noddy's steering wheel.

When Big-Ears and Noddy heard the CLIP-CLOP of Mr Straw's horse, they came rushing outside.

"Go away, cow!" shouted Noddy. "Why are YOU here?"

"She followed you through the open gate," explained Mr Straw. "But I wonder, why is she so fond of you, Noddy?"

Noddy scratched his chin and shook his head. JINGLE.

As soon as the cow heard Noddy's bell, she bounded towards him and tried to pull the hat from Noddy's head.

"It's your BELL she likes!" laughed Mr Straw.

"I will buy her one of her own," said Noddy. "Then she won't need to follow me any more!"

"**MOO!**" said the cow, with pleasure.

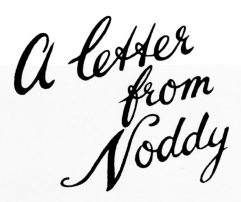

A letter from Noddy

Hallo, all you boys and girls!

I'm little Noddy. You all know me, don't you? I've got a nodding head and that's why I'm called Noddy. Would you like a head like that? I like mine.

I have a dear little car of my very own. I take my friends about in it – the Tubby Bears, who live next door to me, and Miss Fluffy Cat and Mr Jumbo and Mr Wobbly-Man and all the rest. My very best friend of all is Big-Ears. I do love him. He's a good friend because he always helps me when I get into trouble. He's a brownie, and he lives in his Toadstool House up in the woods.

You can share in our adventures and even meet Father Christmas in this very special story collection. I do hope you will like it. Wishing you all a very happy Christmas.

Love from *Noddy*

NODDY FEELS COLD

"Oh dear!" said Noddy, "I wanted to make a nice fire, because I'm so cold – but I've no firewood! Never mind, I'll go and ask Mrs Tubby Bear next door to give me some." So he went to knock at her door.

"Please Mrs Tubby, will you give me a little firewood?" asked Noddy.

"Yes, if you will do something for me," she said. "Go and ask Sally Skittle to let me have some mint out of her garden!" So away went Noddy to Sally Skittle's house.

"Please, Sally Skittle, may I pick some mint?" he asked.

"Well, you must do something for me!" said Sally. "Look – I've broken my teapot. I know Miss Fluffy Cat has two. You go and ask her to lend me one."

Noddy went to Miss Fluffy Cat's house and knocked at the door. She came to open it and smiled at Noddy.

"Please, Miss Fluffy Cat, would you lend me one of your teapots for Sally Skittle?" said Noddy.

"Well, you can take one of these," said Miss Fluffy Cat. "Which would you like – the big one or the small one?"

"The large one, please, because Sally has so many skittle children," said Noddy. "May I take it, Miss Fluffy Cat?"

"Well, do a little errand for me first," said Miss Fluffy Cat. "I want to borrow a ladder. So will you go to Mr Jumbo and ask for his? He always lends it to me when I want it."

"Oh dear!" said Noddy. "What a lot of errands I seem to be doing! And all because I want some firewood!"

He went to Mr Jumbo's. Mr Jumbo lived quite a long way away, down a long lane and over a hill.

And when Noddy got there, Mr Jumbo was out! But Mrs Jumbo was in, and was pleased to see Noddy.

"Oh, you want our ladder?" she said. "Certainly, Noddy – but be a good little fellow, please, and go next door and ask Mrs Little Doll for some pegs for my clothes-line. I haven't enough."

So off Noddy went again, and asked Mrs Little Doll to lend him some pegs for Mrs Jumbo.

"Of course, Noddy," said Mrs Little Doll. "But please do something for me – take my dog and give him a little run, will you? I'm too busy today." So Noddy took her little dog and went for a walk with him. When they got back to Mrs Little Doll's house, they were quite out of breath.

"Thank you, Noddy! Here are the pegs," said Mrs Little Doll. Noddy took them and went back to Mrs Jumbo.

"Here are the pegs you wanted," he said. "Now may I please borrow your ladder, Mrs Jumbo?"

"There it is," said Mrs Jumbo, and off went Noddy with the big ladder – dear me, how heavy it was!

He took it to Miss Fluffy Cat's and she was pleased.

"Thank you, Noddy," she said. "Now here is the large teapot."

Noddy took the large teapot and carried it very carefully indeed to Sally Skittle's house.

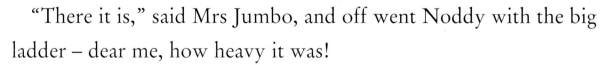

"Thank you, Noddy," said Sally Skittle. "Go and pick some mint." So Noddy picked a nice bunch of mint and took it to Mrs Tubby Bear's. On his way, he smelt it – it really did smell nice and he put some in his button-hole. Soon he arrived at Mrs Tubby Bear's.

"Here is the mint," he said. "Is there enough?"

"Oh, plenty," said Mrs Tubby Bear. "Thank you, Noddy. Now what was it you said you wanted?"

"Some firewood, please," said Noddy, sitting down and mopping his head with his hanky.

"You *do* look hot, Noddy," said Mrs Tubby Bear. "Whatever have you been doing?"

"I've been rushing round all over the place!" said Noddy, "and I'm hot and out of breath!"

"Then why do you want to make yourself a fire?" asked Mrs Tubby Bear, giving him a bundle of wood.

"Oh dear – I don't think I do," said Noddy, giving it back. "I just want an ice-cream now, I'm so hot!" So off Noddy went to buy one. Funny little Noddy – wanting a fire and now going to buy an ice-cream!

NODDY AND THE LITTLE DOLLS

"Noddy – will you take my nine little doll children out for a picnic?" Mrs Jolly-Doll said to him one day. "They are very small, and could quite easily squeeze into your car. Take them to Windy Woods. It's nice there."

"I'd love to," said Noddy, who dearly loved a picnic. "We'll go tomorrow."

"I'll get the picnic basket ready," said Mrs Jolly-Doll. "And I'll put plenty in for you, too, kind little Noddy."

So next day Noddy went to fetch all the little dolls. They were very excited. Mrs Jolly-Doll helped them all into the car, and then put the picnic basket under Noddy's feet, which made it very awkward for him to drive.

"Oh dear – I'll have to drive with my knees knocking into my nose," said Noddy. "Now, are we all ready?"

"Noddy, please bring everyone back safely!" said Mrs Jolly-Doll. "There are ten of you. So, before you get into the car to come back, please count round and see that you have the right number. Can you count up to ten?"

"Oh *yes*," said Noddy. "One, two, three, four, five, six, seven, eight, nine, ten."

"Very clever," said Mrs Jolly-Doll. "Goodbye, and have a good time!"

Noddy drove off. He felt very happy. He liked the little dolls, and they liked him. He felt rather big, because they were so small, and it was very nice to feel big for a change.

They came to Windy Woods. Out they all got and had a game of hide-and-seek before lunch. Then Noddy undid the basket, and, my word, what a fine picnic they had! Egg sandwiches, tomato sandwiches, banana sandwiches. Chocolate biscuits, ginger biscuits. Fruit cake and ginger cake. Lemonade and orangeade. What a feast!

They played games again afterwards, but they all liked hide-and-seek best of all. Then Noddy asked a little bird the time.

"I don't know – except that it's time for you to go home," said the robin. "The sun is going down."

"Come along then, all of you!" cried little Noddy. "Get into the car. Oh, wait though. I must count you first to make sure that all ten of us are here!"

So he made the little dolls stand in a ring and he counted them. "One, two, three, four, five, six, seven, eight, nine. Oh my – there ought to be *ten* of us! Let me count again slowly. One-two-three-four-five-six-seven-eight-nine. There's only nine."

"Where's the tenth?" said a little doll, looking as if she were going to cry. "Is she lost at hide-and-seek?"

"She must be," said Noddy, and a great hunt began. But nobody else could be found. Noddy counted once more. "One, two, three, four, five, six, seven, eight, nine."

They all packed into his car, because by now it was getting dark. Noddy felt very upset. Whatever would Mrs Jolly-Doll say to him?

How dreadful to bring back only nine people, instead of ten.

They got to Mrs Jolly-Doll's house, and Mrs Jolly-Doll came out to welcome them. Noddy helped everyone out, feeling gloomier and gloomier. Oh dear – now he would *have* to tell Mrs Jolly-Doll the bad news.

"Mrs Jolly-Doll," he began. "I'm so very very sorry – but I'm afraid one of us is missing. I only counted nine, you see, instead of ten. But I'll go straight back to the woods and hunt all night long, I will really."

"You must have made a mistake in your counting, Noddy," said Mrs Jolly-Doll. "They all seem to be here."

"No, they're not. You listen to me counting them," said Noddy, and he stood the little dolls round him once more. "One, two, three, four, five, six, seven, eight, nine – there – one missing, you see!"

"But Noddy dear, you forgot to count *yourself!*" said Mrs Jolly-Doll. "See, *I'll* count you all – yourself, too. Listen. One, two, three, four, five, six, seven, eight, nine, TEN! And the tenth is you, little Noddy. You forgot to count yourself!"

"So I did," said Noddy, nodding and smiling. "So I did, aren't I SILLY!"

"Yes – but you're a darling!" said all the little dolls, and they hugged him so hard that he couldn't breathe.

Silly little Noddy! Fancy forgetting to count himself!

WHERE'S YOUR CAR, NODDY?

Now once Toyland was very jolly indeed, because Santa Claus had visited it in his beautiful sleigh. He had driven through it with his fine reindeer, and everyone cheered and clapped.

Santa Claus was the King of Toyland, and all the toys loved him. They put out hundreds of colourful flags. They danced and they sang in the market-place – you can see Noddy dancing with Big-Ears. And you can see Miss Fluffy Cat dancing with Mr Tubby Bear, having a wonderful time.

There were balloons everywhere, tied to the houses, and floating in the air like big coloured bubbles.

"Here come two big balloons, Noddy!" said Big-Ears. "Catch them, quick!"

So Noddy caught them. And then he caught four more, all bright colours and as pretty as could be.

"Tie them to your car, Noddy," said Big-Ears, "and I'll have two to make my bicycle look pretty, too."

Doesn't Noddy's car look fine?

Noddy went off with Big-Ears to get an ice-cream. While he was gone, a wind blew up the street – and it tugged at the balloons on Noddy's car. And, dear me, it tugged so hard that the balloons went up into the air – and took Noddy's car with them!

When Noddy and Big-Ears came back, there was no car to be seen!

"Where's my little car?" wailed Noddy.

"It went off with its balloons," said a skittle. "I saw it go. They floated away with it."

"I must find it, I must!" cried Noddy. "Big-Ears, let's get on your bicycle and go and find it."

On the way, they met two toy rabbits and Noddy asked, "Have you seen a car with balloons?"

"Yes," said the rabbits. "It went over towards the Noah's Ark. We watched it go and one of the balloons burst. You'd better go and find your car because more balloons might burst."

Off went Noddy and Big-Ears on the bicycle. They couldn't see the little car anywhere in the air.

And that wasn't surprising, because, as it floated along, two birds pecked at the balloons – and bang-pop! They all burst and the little car fell down beside the big Noah's Ark.

How surprised the animals were!

"What is it, dropping from the air?" said the bears.

"A car, a car!" cried the giraffe. "I'll drive it. I always wanted to drive a car!"

So the giraffe drove the car, and
then the bears wanted a turn.
As they raced up and down,
they bumped into the elephant,
who was very cross.

"Now then, now then!" he said,
and with his trunk he picked the two
naughty bears out of the car. He tried
to get in himself, but he bent it all to
one side, look! Oh, come quickly, Noddy, before the elephant breaks it
to bits!

Ring r-ring! Here come Noddy and Big-Ears on the bicycle. Noddy
gave such a yell at the elephant.

"What do you think you're doing? Get out at once!" Mr Noah heard
him shout and came out in surprise.

He ordered all the animals to go into the ark – here they go, two by
two – and then he helped Noddy and Big-Ears to put the car right.

"Would you give me a lift?" he said.

So Noddy gave him a lift to Toy Village, and Big-Ears followed on his bicycle.

"Will you stay in the car for a few minutes while I go and speak to Miss Fluffy Cat?" said Noddy to Mr Noah. And, will you believe it, while Noddy was gone, some balloons came bobbing by, near Mr Noah and he caught them and tied them to Noddy's car to make it look pretty. Well, well, well!

He just simply CAN'T understand why Noddy is so cross about it.

"*Silly* Mr Noah!" says Noddy. "I will NOT have balloons on my car any more!"

TESSIE BEAR'S LITTLE STAR

"Tessie dear – go and fetch a pail of water," said Tessie's Auntie Bear one night. "I've spilt some jam on the kitchen floor and I really must wash it off."

Tessie went out into the garden to fetch a pail of water. She let the bucket down into the well, and pulled it up, quite full.

She set it down on the ground – and then looked up at the sky. It was FULL of stars!

"Aren't they pretty?" said little Tessie to herself. "I'd like a necklace of stars. I wonder if any of them ever fall down? I might find one then."

And do you know, JUST as she looked at the starry sky, a bright star rushed down it – and disappeared!

"It left its place! It ran all down the sky! It was the loveliest shooting star I've ever seen!" said Tessie. "I wonder where it fell? Oh, I DO wish I could find it!"

She turned to pick up her bucket – and then how she stared!

"Why! There's a star twinkling up at me from the water!" she cried. "There is, there is! Oh, you dear little star, did you fall into my pail? You must have! One minute you were in the sky – and the next I see you here!"

She looked at the star twinkling in the pail.

"Oh, I can't take you indoors and empty you out on a dirty floor," she said. "I'll catch you in my hand and take you to Noddy. He will like you."

So she put in her hand but of course she couldn't catch the star. That wasn't surprising, because it was only a big star's reflection in the water! Tessie didn't know that.

She picked up the heavy bucket and went to the gate. She meant to walk all the way to Noddy's house with the star in it! Away she went, staggering down the road because the pail was so heavy.

And then Mr Toy-Dog came hurrying up the street and bumped into her – and over went the pail! Splish-splash! Out poured the water!

"Sorry!" called Mr Toy-Dog. "But why carry pails of water at night?"

Tessie Bear was very, very sad. She hunted everywhere for the shining star she had carried in the pail, but she couldn't find it anywhere! She sat down on the kerb and cried.

She wasn't very far from Noddy's house, so she thought she would go and tell him what had happened. Noddy heard a timid little knocking at his door and went to open it. How pleased he was to see little Tessie Bear!

"Come in, Tessie," he said. "But goodness me, why are you carrying an empty pail?"

"When it was full, it had a star in it, Noddy, a star that fell out of the sky," said Tessie. "It was so pretty that I wanted to give it to you."

"Why? For a pet?" said Noddy. "Oh, fancy keeping a star for a pet! Tessie, you are very sweet to come all the way here to bring me a star for a present. But it isn't here – the pail's empty."

"Someone bumped into me and spilt all the water, and the star must have fallen out – I couldn't find it," said Tessie, and she burst into tears again.

Well, Noddy gave her some cocoa and some sugar biscuits and she soon cheered up. Then he took her home and filled her pail at the well again for her.

"Oh look!" he said, when the pail came up full of water again, "LOOK, Tessie – the star is there after all, twinkling away like anything!"

So it was! Noddy darted his hand into the water and tried to catch hold of the star twinkling there – but at that very moment the sky began to cloud over, and hide all the stars. The big black cloud hid the star whose reflection had shone in the water – and because Noddy could no longer see it in the pail, he was sure he must have caught it in his hand. He put it into his pocket at once.

"There, Tessie, I've got it!" he said. "Now you go indoors and don't cry any more. I'll keep your star for ever and ever!"

Do *you* want to see the star that twinkled in Tessie's pail? Then fill a bucket with water on the next starry night, and look down into it. There will be a star there for you too!

NODDY IS QUITE CLEVER

Once when Noddy went to tea with Mrs Tubby, the toy cat was there. Her name was Miss Tibby, and she was quite one of the nicest of the toy cats.

"Good afternoon, Miss Tibby," said Noddy politely. "I hope you're well."

"She's feeling a bit upset," said Mrs Tubby. "She's just discovered a funny thing. She has fine claws in her front paws – but none in her back ones."

"Oh," said Noddy. "Does it matter?"

"Of course it does," said Miss Tibby. "I don't feel a proper toy cat without claws in all my feet. I never noticed it before. One of the dolls laughed at me this morning, and told me, and I was most upset."

"Can't you *buy* claws?" said Noddy.

"You're silly," said the toy cat, and wiped her eyes.

"But you wear shoes," said Noddy. "How did the doll see you hadn't claws?"

"I went to try on some new sandals," said Miss Tibby, "and she noticed when she was trying sandals on my feet. Really, I was dreadfully upset."

"She won't even eat any tea, and I've baked such a lovely chocolate cake," said Mrs Tubby. "I think I won't cut it today, if you are sure you won't have any, Miss Tibby. I'll keep it for tomorrow."

Noddy didn't like hearing that a bit, because he knew he wasn't going to tea with Mrs Tubby tomorrow. It meant he wouldn't have a piece of the lovely cake.

He sat staring mournfully out into Mrs Tubby's pretty little garden.

The roses were out, and looked beautiful. And then, quite suddenly, Noddy's face began beaming, and he stood up.

"Please can I get down for a minute?" he said. "I've thought of an idea."

He went out into the garden to the rose-trees. He looked at each one. He chose one that had very very sharp prickles all the way down the stem.

"You'll do nicely," he said. He broke off ten sharp curved thorns, and took them carefully back to Mrs Tubby's house.

"What *have* you been doing?" asked Mrs Tubby. "Smelling every rose, I should think!"

"I've brought something for Miss Tibby," said Noddy, and he put the curved prickles on her plate. "Claws! Fine, sharp, scratchy claws, just like the ones she has in her front paws. Would they do for your back paws, Miss Tibby?"

"*Well,*" said Miss Tibby in astonishment, "what wonderful claws! Where did you buy them?"

"I didn't," said Noddy. "I broke them off Mrs Tubby's rose-trees. You don't mind, do you, Mrs Tubby?"

"Not a bit. Why, you can be quite clever, Noddy!" said Mrs Tubby. "Look, I am going to cut you a very very very big slice of my chocolate cake; just because I am so pleased with you!"

So Miss Tibby got her claws and Noddy got his chocolate cake, and they were both very happy.

Noddy and the Wooden Horse

Now once when Noddy was driving along a country road, his car suddenly made a peculiar noise, and then stopped.

"Good gracious! What's wrong with you?" said Noddy, in alarm, and he got out to see. "Your wheels haven't got a puncture, and you've plenty of petrol. Then WHY don't you go?"

"Parp-parp," said the car, dolefully, and gave a little rattle.

"I'll have to take you to the garage and get you mended," said Noddy. "Something has gone wrong. But dear me, I'll have to push you all the way because this is a very lonely road and there's nobody to help me."

So he began to push and push, and how he panted and puffed.

"I sound like an engine going up a hill!" said Noddy. "Oh dear, I shall never get you to the garage!"

He pushed the car round the corner of the lane, and then he

suddenly heard a noise. "Hrrrrrumph! Help! Hrrrrumph!"

"Now what can *that* be?" said Noddy, and he stood and listened.

"Nay-hay-hay-hay-hay! Hrrrrrumph! Help!"

"Why – it's a horse in trouble!" said Noddy, and he squeezed through the hedge to find it. Sure enough, in the field beyond was a small horse, neighing and snorting loudly.

"What's the matter?" called Noddy.

"I walked into this muddy bit," said the horse, "and look – my front legs have sunk down into the mud and I can't get them out!"

Noddy ran to help him. "I'll pull you out!" he said. "What part of you shall I pull?"

"My tail," said the horse. "It's a very strong tail. Hold hard – pull. PULL! Pull HARDER. I'm coming. I'm coming!"

Noddy pulled hard at the wooden horse's tail, and, quite suddenly, the horse's front legs came out of the mud, and the horse sat down hard on Noddy.

"Oooh, don't!" said Noddy. "I'm squashed to nothing. Get up, wooden horse. Don't sit on me like this."

"Sorry," said the horse, and got up. "You really are very kind. It was lucky for me that you came by just then in your car."

"Yes, it was," said Noddy. "But I wasn't *in* my car. Something's gone wrong with it, and I've got to push it all the way into Toyland Village. Goodness, I shall be tired!"

"You needn't be," said the wooden horse. "I am quite used to pulling carts. I could pull your car for you, if you like, all the way to the garage! I'd be glad to do you a good turn, little Noddy."

"Oh *thank* you!" said Noddy. "How lucky I am! Come along – I'll get my ropes and tie you to the car. What fun!"

So off they went with Noddy sitting in his car, steering it carefully, and the little wooden horse walking in front, pulling it well. How everyone stared!

"Aren't I lucky?" called little Noddy. "My car broke down – and I found a little wooden horse to pull it!"

"You *are* lucky, Noddy – but, you see, you're kind too, and kind people are *always* lucky!"

NODDY AND THE RED GOBLINS

"Listen, Noddy – if you go through the Goblin Wood in the evening, DON'T stop, whatever happens!" said Big-Ears.

" Oh. But why ever not?" said Noddy, surprised.

"Because the red goblins are about again and you know what tricks they get up to," said Big-Ears. "They'd love to have your car, Noddy – so DO NOT stop for anything if you go through the Goblin Wood."

"But suppose someone hails me and wants to be taken somewhere?" said Noddy.

"Don't stop even for that," said Big-Ears. "It may be a trick."

"All right," said Noddy. "But it does seem rather silly, Big-Ears."

"Now *you're* being rather silly, Noddy," said Big-Ears, crossly. "I'm only trying to help you."

Well, Noddy was very good. He did as Big-Ears told him, and whenever he drove through the Goblin Wood for anything he wouldn't stop for a moment, no matter how the goblins tried to make him.

First they pretended that they wanted to hire his car, and they stood by the roadside, signalling to him – but he drove straight on.

Then two of them walked right in the very middle of the road, thinking *that* would make him stop. But Noddy drove top speed at them, yelling out loudly, "Look out, LOOK OUT, I can't stop,

I CAN'T STOP!"

And the two red goblins hopped out of the way very quickly indeed. They were very angry because they couldn't get Noddy to stop. They did so badly want his car.

Then they thought of a good trick.

"Look!" said one. "I'll blow up this paper bag – and, just as Noddy goes by, I'll hide behind a tree and pop it – BANG – and he'll think he's got a puncture and stop to see."

"Oh good – then we'll all rush out and take his car and go off in it!" said another.

Well, it was a very good trick indeed.
Noddy came along quite fast in his car that
evening, keeping a sharp look-out for the
goblins – but he didn't see a single one.

They were all well hidden! One of
them was behind a tree close to the road,
and when he heard Noddy's car coming,
he blew up his big paper bag – and then he popped it – BANG!

Noddy was just driving by, and he put on his brakes at once and
stopped. "Goodness – that sounded like a puncture in one of my tyres!"
he said, and got out to see. He forgot all about Big-Ears' warning.

In a trice the red goblins were on him. They rolled him in the dust
and then they clambered into the car, and away they went, leaving little
Noddy howling all by himself!

"Big-Ears, oh Big-Ears, why didn't I remember what you said," wept
poor Noddy, getting up and beginning to walk down the long, long
road.

It took him a good time to get to Big-Ears' Toadstool House, and he was crying bitterly when he knocked at the door.

Big-Ears opened it, and Noddy went inside. "Oh, Big-Ears, I stopped on the Goblin Wood road – I thought I had a puncture but I hadn't – and all the goblins rolled me in the dust and drove away in my little car. Oh Big-Ears, I'm so-o-o-o miserable!" Big-Ears put his arms round Noddy.

"I've been waiting for you to come to me," he said. "I knew you'd be along sooner or later."

"How did you know?" wept Noddy. "Oh, Big-Ears, my dear little car will be so unhappy. It will never come back. I'll never see it again. Oh, those wicked red goblins, I wish they could be punished."

Big-Ears laughed. "Don't you worry!" he said. "They have been punished already. Badly punished. And your little car is quite all right."

"Oh, Big-Ears – how do you know all this?" cried Noddy, surprised. "Who told you? What's happened?"

"I'll tell you what has happened," said Big-Ears, "but please stop crying tears all down my waistcoat, or else I really must get an umbrella. Cheer up, Noddy!"

"I'm cheering up," said Noddy, and he gave Big-Ears a very small smile. "Now, tell me."

"Well, your little car was very, very angry when the goblins drove it away," said Big-Ears. "So instead of driving off to their town as they wanted it to, it drove itself straight to the big duck-pond – and it stopped right on the very edge – and all the goblins shot straight up into the air and fell SPLASH into the water!"

"Oh! Oh, isn't my car clever!" cried Noddy, and he laughed and laughed. "What a shock for the red goblins! What happened next?"

"Nothing much except that the car came straight here to wait for you," said Big-Ears. "It's outside now, but you were crying so much you didn't see it. Call it!"

"Car! Little car!" shouted Noddy in delight. And from outside came the sound Noddy knew so well.

"Parp-parp! Parp-parp-parp!"

Well done, little car – you deserve a very good polish all over – and Noddy will see that you get it!

Ho-Ho-Ho-Ho!

O ne morning, when Noddy had driven the farmer's wife to market and back, she gave him twelve new-laid eggs for himself.

"Oooh, thank you!" said Noddy. "I do so like an egg for breakfast! There's enough here for Tessie Bear too."

But Tessie was away, so Noddy thought he would share them with old Big-Ears. He drove up to the Toadstool House and knocked at the door.

No one opened it. Bother! Big-Ears must be out. Noddy opened the door and went in. No – Big-Ears was there – but he was fast asleep in his chair, quite tired out with all the gardening he had done!

He had put his hat on the table beside him, and taken off his shoes. Noddy smiled and was careful not to nod his head in case his bell rang and wakened Big-Ears.

"I'll give him a nice surprise," thought Noddy.
"I'll pop six eggs inside his hat – and when he
wakes up, he *will* be pleased to see them!
He can fry some for his dinner."

So Noddy carefully put six of the biggest
eggs into Big-Ears' hat, and then tiptoed out
of the room. Away he went in his car, thinking
how surprised Big-Ears would be to find eggs
inside his hat.

Big-Ears woke up at last – and jumped up at once when he saw how
late it was. He caught up his red hat and jammed it on his head...

Ooooooh! Whatever was this trickling all down his neck? Big-Ears
put up his hand to feel – and his fingers came away covered with
yellow egg-yolk! He tore off his hat and looked inside.

"Eggs! Eggs in my hat! All smashed to bits
when I put it on my head! Look at it – and
look at my clothes! COVERED with
yellow egg-yolks! Ruined! Who did this?

WHO DID IT, I say! Wait till I get hold of him! I'll complain to Mr Plod! I'll go this very minute!"

But poor Big-Ears couldn't go in his eggy clothes. They looked dreadful, and were sticky with yolk wherever he touched them. So he took them off and put on a clean set of clothes. Away he went on his bicycle, with no hat, as angry as could be. Wait till Mr Plod hears about this! Perhaps it was that bad little Tricky Teddy who had played such a trick.

Now Noddy had to go past Big-Ears' house in the afternoon, on his way back from Rocking-Horse Town.

"I'll just pop in and see if he liked the eggs," he said. "Perhaps he will ask me to tea."

So in he went – and the very first thing he saw was Big-Ears' hat, all messed with broken eggs. Then he saw Big-Ears' other clothes on the ground, all yellow and sticky too. Noddy sat down suddenly in a chair, feeling very scared. He guessed at once what had happened.

"Oh DEAR! I never thought he'd put his hat on without looking inside. Oh DEAR, DEAR, DEAR! Now I'm going to get into terrible trouble. Oh, I'm so sorry, so very sorry. What shall I do?"

Then an idea came to him. He picked up the eggy hat and clothes, and drove home with them as fast as ever he could. He meant to wash them at once, and get them clean for poor old Big-Ears.

My goodness, how well he washed them! Soon he was pegging them out on the line in the wind, and then went indoors to make some tea – and at that very minute he heard the sound of Big-Ears' bicycle bell!

"Oh – now he's going to be so cross!" said poor Noddy, and opened the door to let in Big-Ears. Big-Ears began to tell him at once about the eggs.

"I've been to Mr Plod," he said, "and told him I'm sure it was Tricky Teddy, and..."

And then he looked out of the window and saw all his clothes dancing about in the wind on Noddy's line! He was so surprised that he couldn't say a word!

"Oh Big-Ears, dear Big-Ears, I put the eggs into your hat for a *present*," said Noddy. "And I was DREADFULLY sorry when I saw what had happened. So I took all your things back to wash. Please, please, Big-Ears, don't take me to Mr Plod."

Well, Big-Ears didn't. He stared at little Noddy as he spoke – and then his face wrinkled up, and his mouth opened wide – and out came the biggest laugh that Noddy had ever heard!

"HO-HO-HO-HO-HO! I might have guessed! HO-HO-HO-HO! Who else but you would be so kind and so SILLY, Noddy! You'll make me die of laughing, you really will! HO-HO-HO-HO-HO!"

A HOLE IN HIS POCKET

"Oh dear!" said Noddy, "I do believe there's a teeny little hole in my pocket! Yes, there is. I *must* remember to mend it. I'll do it after my breakfast."

But he didn't. He felt the hole again and thought that really it was so very small nothing could fall through it.

"I'll mend you tonight, hole," said Noddy. But the hole didn't stay small. It grew bigger, and when Noddy began to put sixpences and shillings into his pocket, as passengers paid him for riding in his little car, the hole grew bigger still.

Noddy forgot all about it. He felt very very pleased with himself as he drove home that evening. He jingled his money and made up his mind to go and buy little Tessie Bear and dear old Big-Ears a present each the very next day.

When he got home he washed himself, and sat down to a very late tea. How hungry he was! He ate all the cakes in his tin, and half a loaf of bread, and butter and honey.

"And now I'll go and dig my garden," he said. "I feel just like digging. Where's my spade?"

Well, he dug and he dug, and grew very hot indeed. Mrs Tubby Bear looked over the fence and laughed.

"You're as red as one of the apples on my tree!" she said. "Come over and pick one, and tell me your news while you have a rest."

Noddy was pleased. He went into Mrs Tubby Bear's garden, and picked himself a fine apple. Then he sat down to tell her his news.

"I had a very, very busy day, Mrs Tubby Bear," he said. "And I made a lot of money!"

"Did you now?" said Mrs Tubby Bear, going on with her knitting. "And what are you going to spend it on?"

"Well, tomorrow, the very first thing I shall do is to buy Big-Ears a new book to read," said Noddy. "He's read his old one eighty-two times, he says – so it's time he had a new one, isn't it?"

"It certainly is," said Mrs Tubby.

"And then I'm going to buy little Tessie Bear a jar of honey," said Noddy. "She loves honey. All bears do. Did you know that, Mrs Tubby?"

"Well, yes, I did," said Mrs Tubby, smiling. "You see, I've been a bear myself for a very long time, Noddy."

"Oh yes. I forgot," said Noddy. "Well, you are so very nice, Mrs Tubby, that I shall buy *you* a present too. Let me count my money – then you'll see what a lot I've got." He put his hand into his pocket – and then he gave such a howl that Mrs Tubby almost dropped her knitting.

"My money! It's gone!" cried Noddy, and tears began to run down his cheeks. "I had a hole in my pocket, and I didn't mend it. My money has dropped out, every bit of it. Now I shan't be able to buy *anyone* a present."

"Oh, Noddy, Noddy, you little silly!" said Mrs Tubby. "But surely you would have *heard* it drop out, clinkity-clink? Yes, surely you would."

"I didn't, I didn't," wept Noddy. "Oh, why didn't I?"

"Well then – the money must have dropped on something so soft that you didn't hear it," said Mrs Tubby. "On a soft carpet – or grass – or... OH! I know where your money will be, Noddy!"

"Where?" asked Noddy, wiping his eyes.

"Where you were *digging*, of course!" said Mrs Tubby. "It must have dropped out then; every time you drove your spade into the ground you must have jerked out money! And you didn't hear it because it fell into the soft earth!"

"Oh, Mrs Tubby – you *are* clever!" said Noddy. "I'll go and look, now, at once, this very minute!"

And over the wall he went into his own little garden. There in the earth, just as Mrs Tubby said, was every bit of his money! Oh, how happy Noddy was! He picked it all up – and put it into his pocket!

But that was silly, wasn't it! Mrs Tubby scolded him. "There you go again, little Noddy, using that hole in your pocket! Fetch a needle and cotton, come back here, and I'll mend it for you!"

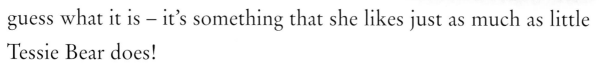

So now it's mended and his money is safe – and the very *first* present he buys tomorrow morning is going to be for Mrs Tubby! You can guess what it is – it's something that she likes just as much as little Tessie Bear does!

(*Noddy says, if you're not very clever at guessing, well, it rhymes with* MONEY)

FATHER CHRISTMAS
COMES TO TOYLAND

One morning Big-Ears came knocking at Noddy's little front door in great excitement.

"I've got some very exciting news, Noddy," said Big-Ears. "Father Christmas is coming next week in his sleigh, with four reindeer. He's staying the night with my brother, Little-Ears."

"Goodness! What an honour!" said Noddy, feeling very excited too. "Shall I be able to see Father Christmas?"

"Well, my brother, Little-Ears, has asked me to his house on the night that Father Christmas is there," said Big-Ears, "and I thought you could take me in your car, Noddy, and sing a song outside the house while Father Christmas is having his supper!"

"Oh, Big-Ears! Oh, what a wonderful idea!" said Noddy, almost falling off his chair in excitement. "Oh, I'll make my car look simply beautiful."

At last the big day arrived and everyone was up very early. Noddy gave his car one last polish. It really looked magnificent. He tied a big bow in front, in the middle of the bumper.

The car was so pleased with itself, it hooted, "Parp-parp-PARP!"

Noddy took off his overall and went to wash himself and dress. He even polished up the bell on the top of his blue hat.

The roadway had to be cleared for Father Christmas' arrival, because the sleigh and the four reindeer took up rather a lot of room. Noddy put his car safely in the garage, but he left the door open so that the car could join in the excitement and hoot at the right time.

Noddy went to stand at his gateway and Big-Ears came along on his bicycle.

The noise of the bells grew louder and louder. JING-JING-JING-JINGLE-JING! JINGLE-JING! And then Noddy saw the reindeer coming up the road. How lovely they looked with their great antlers growing from their heads! JING-JING-JINGLE-JING. And there was Father Christmas in his sleigh, smiling all over his big red face, and his blue eyes twinkling all the time. He waved his hand to everyone, and his red cloak flew out in the wind behind him.

Noddy gave a big sigh.

"Never mind," said Big Ears, "you might get a peep at him tonight, but that's all, little Noddy. He's a Most Important Person, you know."

"Yes, I do know. It's what my song says," said little Noddy, his head nodding up and down. "I'm glad my song is going to be sung outside Little-Ears' house tonight."

That evening Mr Tubby arranged the singers in a row. Noddy stood in the front, suddenly feeling very shy. Everyone looked at him, and

Noddy raised a little twig he had found in a ditch.

"OH...!" sang everyone, and then went on with the song.

"There's a Most Important Person

That I hope we're going to see..."

Right on to the end of the song they all went, and you should have heard how they shouted out Father Christmas' name when they came to it in the song!

The door opened – and out came the Most Important Person himself!

He smiled round at everyone and his blue eyes twinkled brightly.

"Very nice indeed," he said. "And may I ask which of you wrote that extremely good song?"

"Noddy did," said Miss Fluffy, and she pushed Noddy towards Father Christmas. "He's our taxi-driver and he often makes up songs."

"Dear me – so this is little Noddy!" said Father Christmas. He put out his hand and Noddy shook it, very red in the face.

"So you're a taxi-driver, are you?" said Father Christmas. "Where's your car?"

"Here," said Noddy, finding his tongue, and waved his hand towards his little car.

"Parp-parp," said the car, and put its lights on and off all by itself.

"What a dear little car!" said Father Christmas. "And how beautifully clean and shiny! Dear me, I wish I could travel through Toyland in this instead of going in my bumpy old sleigh."

"Oh," said Noddy, going even redder than ever, "please have my car while you are here in Toyland. It's very easy to drive."

"That's kind of you," said Father Christmas, "but it would be a change for me to be driven instead of driving myself. I suppose you wouldn't like to come with me and drive me where I want to go?"

Noddy lost his tongue again. He couldn't say a single word! He just stared at Father Christmas as if he couldn't believe his ears.

"Oh," said Noddy, sitting down suddenly. "Oh! I must be dreaming!" But he wasn't – it was quite, quite true!

Next morning Noddy was outside Little-Ears' house at exactly nine o'clock. Out came Father Christmas.

"Now, let me see," he said, taking out a fat notebook. "I want to go to Bouncing Ball Village. I hear that some of the balls I gave to the children last year hadn't got much bounce in them. I must enquire into that."

Off they went, Noddy feeling as proud as could be. His bell jingled all the time.

"You sound like a small reindeer, jingling like that!" said Father Christmas, and gave one of his enormous laughs.

"Hallo – are we in Bouncing Ball Village so soon? Good. Call the Chief Bouncer to me, will you?"

Little balls came bouncing round to see who had come. When they saw it was Father Christmas they bounced in excitement, trying to jump right over the car.

The Chief Bouncer was an enormous coloured ball, the kind that likes to be played with at the seaside. He listened to Father Christmas and then he promised to see that every ball in the village should have proper bouncing lessons before being sent to the world of boys and girls.

"Now go to Teddy Town," said Father Christmas. "I've had very good reports from boys and girls about their teddy bears – they love them very much. I want to give some praise there."

On they went to Teddy Town. The Chief Teddy was very proud to see Father Christmas.

"You are training your teddy bears well," said Father Christmas. "I am pleased with you. One little girl has asked for a tiny doll's house teddy bear. Can you do anything about that?"

"Certainly, Father Christmas," said the Chief Teddy.

On they went, and the little car behaved beautifully. It didn't knock any lamp-posts down, it didn't go into any puddles, and it ran round bumps in the road instead of jolting over them.

It was a very exciting day. Noddy felt so proud to be driving Father Christmas. He felt prouder still to be sitting at a table and having tea with him, and he was very pleased to find that Father Christmas liked ice-creams as much as he did!

They slept in Humming-Top Village that night, and all night long there was the humming of excited tops who couldn't go to sleep because Father Christmas had come to visit them.

Next day off they went again. They went to Wooden-Engine Village, and Noddy had time to drive one. He had always wanted to do that. And he was so excited that he really drove it much too fast!

Noddy was very sorry when it was time to go home.

"We'll have a party when we get back," Father Christmas said to Noddy. "I feel like a party, Noddy. Do you?"

"Oh, yes – I always feel like a party – just like I always feel like an ice-cream," said Noddy.

Big-Ears was very pleased to see Noddy safely home again and to hear from Father Christmas what a splendid little driver he had been.

"We're going to have a party," said Noddy. "Will you and Little-Ears arrange it, Big-Ears?"

"You shall have one tomorrow!" said Big-Ears, beaming. "In the market-place, so that everyone can come. I'll get the big town-bell and go and call out the news."

"DINGA-DONG! DINGA-DONG! News! NEWS! NEWS!"

Well, it wasn't long before everyone heard the news that Father Christmas and little Noddy were safely back and were going to have a party. Goodness me, what excitement there was!

The reindeer were asked to the party, too, and Little-Ears spent a long time polishing their antlers for them. In fact, everyone was asked, even the bunnies in the woods.

The party began at three o'clock, and there was so much to eat that the tables that stood in the middle of the market-place creaked under the weight of it all.

Father Christmas sat at the top of the table and Noddy sat on his right-hand-side, feeling so proud that he could hardly speak a word.

But his bell rang all the time, and his little car, parked nearby, hooted.

"Jingle-parp, parp-jingle-jing, parple, parple-parple, jingle-jing!"

Father Christmas got up and made a speech.

"I don't make long speeches," he said, "but I do want to say that Noddy is one of the nicest, kindest little toys I've ever met, and quite the best driver!"

"Hooray! Hooray!" cried everyone.

"Speech, Noddy, speech!" shouted Mr and Mrs Tubby. Noddy began to tremble. "I don't know what to say," said little Noddy. "I-I don't-know-" And suddenly he stood up straight and smiled.

"It's all right!" he said. "I'll sing a song instead!"

And here is the song that he sang at that wonderful party:

"I'm only little Noddy
Who's got a song to sing,
And a little car to ride in,
And a bell to jingle-jing.
I've a little house to live in
And a little garage too.
But I've something BIG inside me,
And that's my love for YOU –
My love for ALL of you!"

Much better than a speech, little Noddy. No wonder everyone is clapping and cheering you. Well done!

A letter from Noddy

Hallo, Boys and Girls,

Guess who I am? Yes, I'm little Noddy, and if you come to Toy Town where I live, you will always know when I'm coming because my blue hat has a bell on the top which goes jingle-jingle-jing.

If you want to visit me I live in my dear little house of bricks called "House-for-One". Next door live Mr and Mrs Tubby Bear and they are very kind to me. I have a little red and yellow car of my own because I'm a taxi driver and I work very hard. Sometimes I go to the wood to see my dear friend Big-Ears the Brownie. He lives in a Toadstool House with his cat and he has a bicycle with a bell on it.

You can meet more of my friends and share in our many adventures in my story collection. I hope you will enjoy it. Now I will sign my name in my Very Best Writing.

Love from

Noddy

What a Thing to Happen

Once Noddy had a bear on wheels for a passenger. He was a nice bear, but because he was on wheels he found it rather difficult to sit in the car.

"I'm not sure I want you for a passenger," said Noddy, at last, after he had spent five minutes trying to fix the bear in safely. "You'll scratch my car with your wheels."

"Oh, please do take me," said the bear. "I've got to go and have my growl seen to. It's gone wrong. I do beg of you to take me, because I'm not allowed on the bus."

"All right," said Noddy, "I'll take you. But really you are a most awkward passenger to fit in!" They set off at last.

The bear wanted to go to Bear Town and that was quite a long way off. And, dear me, halfway there something peculiar happened!

When Noddy drove over a big bump in the road one of the wheels flew off his little car! It came right off and rolled at top speed down the hill behind them. The car gave a jolt and came to a stop on only three wheels.

"Oh, I say! A wheel's gone!" said Noddy, looking scared. "What am I to do?"

"Go after it," said the bear. "I'll get out and look too. You can ride on my back if you like because I can run very quickly downhill on my four big wheels."

So Noddy got on the bear's furry back and away they went down the hill to look for the lost wheel. But they couldn't find it anywhere! It had quite disappeared.

"Fallen in the river, I suppose, or been eaten by a goat," said the bear.

"Do goats eat wheels?" said Noddy, in surprise. "Oh, I shall never like goats again."

They went back to the car. "Well, we'll have to leave my poor little car here all by itself because its spare wheel is at the garage, being mended," said Noddy, with tears in his eyes. "It won't like being left. It'll miss its own garage."

"I've got an idea," said the bear, "but I don't know if you'll think it's a very good one. I suppose you wouldn't like me to lend you one of *my* wheels, would you? They're about the same size as the car's wheels, and one of mine might just do for it till the other wheel is found or you get a new one."

"Well, what a wonderful idea!" cried Noddy. He undid one of the bear's wheels, and he and the bear together fitted it on the car. It wasn't quite the same size, but it did very well indeed.

"The car goes along rather jerkily," said Noddy, "but, anyway, it *goes*! You really are a clever bear. I'm so glad I took you for a passenger after all."

"Yes, you were kind, and kindness is always a very good thing," said the bear. "Well, here we are at Bear Town. I'll get my growl put right and then we'll go back. I think I can run on three wheels all right."

He was soon back, with his growl nice and deep again. He growled just to show Noddy how good it was. Then Noddy helped him into the car again and off they went.

"You'd better come and have some lemonade and buns with me," said Noddy, when they got back. "Bears do like buns, don't they?"

"Oh yes," said the bear, pleased. So Noddy drove the little car to his house - and there, leaning by the front gate, was the lost wheel! Noddy stared at it in wonder and delight.

"Somebody brought your wheel back for you," said Mr Tubby, the bear, looking out of one of his windows. "I told him to put it there, and I gave him a penny for bringing it. I say, that's a very odd wheel you've got instead!"

"It may be odd, but it's been very useful!" said Noddy. "Now, bear, you can have your wheel back, and I can put mine on again. What a bit of luck!"

They did enjoy their buns and lemonade. When the bear went he said thank you to Noddy. "And if EVER you want a spare wheel in a hurry again, let me know. I'll always lend you one of mine!" he said.

Wasn't it nice of him!

NODDY IS RATHER CLEVER

One day Mr Noah was worried. He had counted the animals and birds in his Ark, and, dear me, two were missing!

"The two brown bears are gone," he said. "Now what shall I do? How very naughty of them."

He went to tell Mr Plod, and soon everyone knew that the two brown bears had run away from the Ark.

"Just because I said they were to wipe their feet when they came into the Ark after their walk!" said Mrs Noah. "Really, they are too touchy for words!"

"Who's going after them?" said Mr Plod. "I hear they can be rather fierce. I have too much to do today to chase them myself. Look, there's Big-Ears. Perhaps he would go after them. Hey, Big-Ears!"

Big-Ears said he would rush round and about on his little bicycle and see if he could find the bears. "I'll tell Noddy, too," he said. "He is out in his car this morning. He can look out for them."

He found Noddy and told him. Noddy felt rather scared. "But I don't *want* to chase bears," he said. "They are *much* more likely to chase me. And what would I do if I saw them? I might run away."

"Don't be such a little coward," said Big-Ears. "Anyway, you'll be in your car. You'll be quite safe."

He rode away on his bicycle and Noddy went off in his car, hoping that he wouldn't see a single bear. The wooden bears from the Ark always looked rather fierce to him.

And, will you believe it, as he turned a corner, there were the two bears walking down the lane! Noddy was full of alarm. *Now* what was he to do? Should he turn round at top speed and rush away?

No. That wouldn't be at all brave. Big-Ears would be most ashamed of him. Noddy stopped his car and stared at the two brown bears coming towards him. His little knees shook in fright.

And then a Wonderful Idea came into Noddy's head, and the little bell on his hat tinkled loudly. It always did when Noddy had a good idea.

He called to the two brown bears. "Hey! Do you want a lift?"

"Well, we *are* rather tired," said one bear. "Yes, we'd like a lift."

So they both got into the car, and it really was a terrible squash. But the bears seemed very grateful and friendly, so Noddy didn't mind.

He drove off at top speed. Where was Noddy going? Ah, that was his Wonderful Idea!

"I shall drive at top speed to Mr Noah at the Ark!" thought Noddy. "Yes, that's what I shall do. Oh, what a Wonderful Idea!"

Along the lane, and over the bridge, and through the village. Parp-parp-parp went the hooter, and everyone turned and stared.

"Look! There's Noddy! He's caught the two runaway bears!" shouted Big-Ears, wobbling along on his bicycle.

"He's got the bears!" yelled Mr Tubby.

"Isn't he brave?" shouted Mr Plod.

Big-Ears followed on his bicycle. Noddy drove up to the Ark - and there was Mr Noah standing at the door, waiting. He looked very stern.

The bears stared in surprise. "Oh - we've come to the Ark," they said.

"You have," said Mr Noah. "Get out of that car. Go into the Ark at once. And be sure to WIPE YOUR FEET. Then put yourselves to bed in disgrace. I will come and talk to you soon."

The bears hung their heads and shuffled off into the Ark. Big-Ears rode up, panting. He leapt off his bicycle and thumped Noddy on the back.

"You're a wonder!" he said. "You're a marvel! Isn't he, Mr Noah?"

"Yes," said Mr Noah, "and very very brave, too. Noddy, you shall have the biggest ice-cream you've ever seen!"

So he did - and you can see him eating it. Isn't it ENORMOUS!

A-Tishoo!

"A-tish-oooo!" said Noddy suddenly, and tried to catch the sneeze in his hanky.

"You've caught a cold," said Big-Ears.

"I haven't," said Noddy. "I think it must have caught *me*, Big-Ears. Oh dear, I hope I shan't give it to you, too. A-TISH-ooooo!"

"Now, you go to bed, and get a hot-water bottle, and wrap yourself up in a shawl, and have something hot to drink with a lemon in it," said Big-Ears. "You'll soon be better then."

Well, Noddy didn't give his cold to Big-Ears, he gave it away some-where else! He was driving his car along when suddenly it made a most peculiar noise.

"Whooooooooosh-OOOO!" It shook and shivered and Noddy was quite alarmed.

"What are you doing, car? Have you got a puncture in one of your tyres?"

"WHOOOOOSH-OOO!" said the car, even more loudly, and shook and shivered again.

"I believe you're sneezing. I believe you've got a cold," said Noddy anxiously. "Oh dear, oh dear. Well, I must look after you well, because it would never do to have a car that coughed and sneezed all the time. Come along home - I'll put you to bed."

Well, Noddy took his little car home and put it into the garage. He fetched a big blanket and draped it all round it, like a shawl.

"Is that nice and warm?" he said. "Now I'll get you a hot drink with lemon in."

Off he went and boiled a kettle of water and poured it into a jug with hot lemon in it. Then out he went to the garage and put the hot drink into the car's water-tank. It seemed to like it very much.

"Now for a hot-water bottle," said Noddy, and bustled off again. Soon he had the bottle ready and he put it just underneath the car to keep it warm.

"You'll soon be all right,"

he said. "Now keep warm, go to sleep, and wake up better in the morning because we've got a lot of passengers to take out."

Well, the car did go to sleep. It began to snore a little because it was so warm and comfortable. Mr Tubby Bear was coming home late that night and he was most surprised to hear this strange noise coming from Noddy's garage. He peeped down and looked through the keyhole.

And there was the car, fast asleep, warm, comfortable and snoring a little. Mr Tubby couldn't help smiling.

"Dear old Noddy!" he said. "He even tries to make his car comfortable and happy. I suppose it's got a cold! Well, it should be better tomorrow, with all this kind treatment."

It was, of course. It didn't sneeze any more, and it didn't cough once. "There," said Noddy, as he drove away in it to collect his passengers, "see how clever I am, little car! I can even cure your cold!"

128

A Little Mistake

Once little Noddy went to tea with Big-Ears. He drove up to his toadstool house, and hooted loudly.

"Parp-parp!"

Big-Ears came to the door. "Hallo, little Noddy! You're in good time. I've almost got tea ready, and there is a lovely new pot of honey!"

"Oooh!" said Noddy. "I like honey. I wish I were a bee. I'd like to be small enough to go and hunt for honey in the flowers whenever I was hungry."

He went into Big-Ears' little house. It was such a dear little house, and so cosy inside. Noddy loved it. Big-Ears had laid the table, and there was a plate of new bread and butter, a big pot of honey, a round fruit cake and ginger biscuits.

"Now sit down and tell me all your news," said Big-Ears. "Have you had any passengers in your car today?"

"Yes, two," said little Noddy. "One was big Mr Jumbo, and he's so heavy he makes the tyres go quite flat. And the other was Sally Skittle, and two little girl-skittles. Oh dear - one fell out, and Sally Skittle was cross."

"Well, skittles are always falling down," said Big-Ears. "That's what they're meant to do. Look, Noddy - I've spread a whole big slice of bread and butter with honey for you. Here you are."

"Oh, thank you, Big-Ears," said Noddy, and reached out his hand for

for it. "Oh, goodness me - I've put my thumb on the honey. Can I lick it, or is that rude?"

"Get your hanky out, Noddy," said Big-Ears, "I know what you're like with honey! You'll have it all over yourself in a minute!"

Noddy put his hand in his pocket, and pulled out - a letter! He stared at it in surprise.

"This isn't my hanky," he said. "Dear me, where did this letter come from?"

Big-Ears looked at it. "It's addressed to Miss Jane Jumbo," he said. "How odd!"

"Oh, I remember now - oh dear! Mr Jumbo asked me to post it for him!" said Noddy, his head nodding madly. "I forgot. I quite forgot!"

"Then that was very bad of you," said Big-Ears. "If you say you will do something you MUST do it. Now, you go straight out to the little red post-box down the lane, and post that letter right away. No, you can't finish your tea first. Go now."

"All right," said Noddy, seeing that Big-Ears looked quite cross with him. "May I take my piece of bread and butter and honey with me, Big-Ears, please?"

"Yes," said Big-Ears. "Hurry up. I'll wait till you come back before I cut the fruit cake."

Noddy hurried off down the lane, his slice of bread and honey in one hand and the letter in the other.

Big-Ears sat and waited.

And then he heard a noise. What was it? Good gracious, it was Noddy, and he was wailing loudly as he came back from the post. Big-Ears rushed to the door.

"Noddy! What's the matter? Have you hurt yourself?"

"Big-Ears - oh Big-Ears - when I got to the post-box, I - I - I..." wept Noddy.

"Well, go on," said Big-Ears.

"Oh, Big-Ears, I made a mistake - and I posted my bread and honey!" wailed Noddy. "I did, I did! And I made another mistake too. I bit a big piece out of Mr Jumbo's letter. Look!"

Big-Ears looked at the bitten letter. Then he looked at Noddy. "Well, well, well - whatever will you do next?" he said. "Posting bread and honey - and eating letters!"

"Go and get my bread and honey!" wept Noddy.

"I can't because the post-box is locked," said Big-Ears. "You'll have to go and tell the postman you are sorry, when he comes to collect the letters. And you'll have to go and tell Mr Jumbo what you have done, and say you're sorry to him too. He'll have to write another letter."

"But they'll both be so cross with me," said Noddy, and oh dear, he wiped his eyes with Jumbo's letter!

"That's not your hanky!" said Big-Ears. "Noddy, people ought to be cross with you when you're silly. Now, you go straight off to Mr Jumbo's. Hurry! You can have your tea when you come back!"

So there goes poor little Noddy in his car, feeling very sorry for himself. Fancy posting a slice of bread and honey - what a thing to do!

BIG-EARS' RED HAT

Big-Ears always wore a red hat. It fitted him well and had a nice point at the top. He was very proud of it and wore it every day.

One day Noddy called for him in his little car and said he would take him for a ride. "I haven't any passengers today," he said, "so you can come for a little trip with me, Big-Ears. I will show you how fast my little car can go."

Big-Ears was pleased. He got in and Noddy set off through the wood. Parp-parp! Parp-parp! He hooted his horn to make the rabbits get out of the way.

When he got to a hill Noddy went down it very fast indeed. Whoooooosh! Big-Ears felt the wind rushing by his head, and he put up his hand to hold onto his hat.

But alas! It flew right off his head and up into the air! Big-Ears gave a yell.

"Stop, stop, Noddy! Stop, I say!"

"Oh, we can't stop in the middle of a hill," said Noddy, who was really enjoying himself. "It's all right, Big-Ears. Don't be frightened. I'm really a very good driver."

"I'm NOT frightened!" said Big-Ears crossly. "But I want you to STOP. Can't you see that my hat has blown away?"

Noddy turned to look, and was so surprised to see Big-Ears without his red hat that he let the car almost run into a lamp-post. Big-Ears clutched the wheel just in time.

"Noddy! Look where you are going!"

"Well, you told me to look and see that your hat was gone," said Noddy. "I can't look two ways at once. Oh, Big-Ears - your lovely hat!"

135

"Yes. My lovely hat!" said Big-Ears. "I shall never, never get another one to fit my big head. That was specially made for me. How silly you are to go so fast, Noddy."

"We'll go back and look for it," said Noddy, and he turned the car round. Back they went, chugging up the hill. Then Noddy suddenly gave a shout.

"There it is, look - on that bush over there! I'll get it." So out he got, and ran to a clump of bushes. All sorts of things had been draped over them - a blue dress, a pink petticoat, a yellow shawl - but Noddy only had eyes for the little red thing on the smallest bush. He pounced on it.

And then a cross voice called out to him.

"Hey, you little robber! What are you doing, taking my washing! I've just hung it over the bushes to dry. You leave it alone!"

"But it's Big-Ears' hat," said Noddy.

"It is not," said a plump mother-doll running over to him. "It's my red scarf!"

And, dear me, so it was! Noddy shook it out and it wasn't a red hat at all, but just a pretty scarf. He was most surprised. He ran back to the car with the mother-doll after him.

"I'm sorry, I'm sorry, I'm sorry!" he shouted, and drove off at top speed. Big-Ears looked very cross.

"We shall never find my hat," he said. "I don't feel as if I want to speak to you today, Noddy. I'm annoyed with you."

Noddy hated Big-Ears not to speak to him. He looked all round and about for the lost red hat. Ah - there it was, blowing over the grass in a nearby field.

Noddy hopped out of the car and ran to it. The wind played a fine game with him! It blew the red thing here and there, and Noddy went up to his knees in a stream before he caught it.

And it wasn't the hat after all - it was just an old red rag that Mrs Skittle had thrown away on her rubbish-heap.

The wind had taken it to play with.

Noddy went sadly back to the car. Big-Ears didn't say a word. He just sat and stared in front of him. It was really dreadful.

Noddy sighed and started the car again. If only he could find Big-Ears' hat! Then everything would be all right again.

And then he really *did* see a red hat! It was sticking up just over the top of a low hedge. The wind must have taken it there! Noddy leapt out of the car and ran to it. Yes, it really was a red, pointed hat.

He tugged at it and it came easily into his hand. But, dear me, somebody on the other side of the hedge suddenly stood up and looked over the top, very angry indeed. It was Mr Big-Beard, an old brownie.

"Noddy! How DARE you! Snatching my hat off my head just as I was taking a nap under the hedge in the sun! I've a mind to tell Mr Plod. Come here!"

"I'm sorry, I'm sorry, I'm sorry!" wailed poor Noddy. He threw back the hat and ran to the car. Oh dear - what a dreadful thing to happen. And there was Big-Ears, still cross and not saying a word.

"I'll drive you home, Big-Ears," said Noddy, in a very small voice. "This is not my lucky morning."

So he drove Big-Ears slowly home - and, will you believe it, when they got there, there was something red on the top of Big-Ears' chimney. How they stared!

"It's my hat!" said Big-Ears joyfully. "The wind brought it back for me, and because I wasn't in it put it on my chimney where I could see it! Oh, what a lucky thing!"

"I'll get a ladder and take it down for you, dear Big-Ears," said Noddy. "And then you will speak to me nicely again, won't you?"

So he got Big-Ears' red hat for him, and Big-Ears smiled and put it on. Then he put his arm round little Noddy and squeezed him.

"I'm sorry I was cross," he said. "I'm always cross without my hat."

"Then you must never, never lose it again," said Noddy happily. And Big-Ears said he never, never would!

NODDY GETS A FRIGHT

Once Noddy was asked to a party. Sally Skittle asked him, and Noddy was very pleased.

"I'm going to Sam Skittle's party," he told Big-Ears. "His mother asked me if I would. It's his birthday."

"Then you must take him a present," said Big-Ears. "Have you any money in your money-box, Noddy?"

"Oh yes, lots!" said Noddy. "I was saving up to buy myself a nice pair of warm gloves, Big-Ears. My hands do get so cold on these winter days, when I'm driving the car."

Big-Ears tipped out the money from the money-box. "Yes," he said, "you've quite a lot. You can buy the gloves and a birthday present for Sam Skittle, too."

So Noddy bought Sam Skittle a little trumpet, and he bought himself a pair of fine red gloves, very warm indeed.

He felt very proud when he put
them on. They were the first pair he
had had. He thought he would wear
them to the party and drive
himself there in his little car.

"Now - am I all clean and
tidy?" he said to himself
when the party afternoon
came. "Have I washed my
hands and face? Yes, I have.
Have I brushed my hair?
Yes - oh no, I haven't.
Dear me, what a good thing
that I ask myself questions
like these!"

He brushed his hair. He put on
his hat, and the little bell jingled merrily.
He tied up his shoe-laces well and brushed some dust off his shorts.
He put on his nice new gloves and went out to his car.

"I've got new gloves that fit my wooden hands nicely," said Noddy
to his car.

"Parp-parp!" said the car, and off they went. Soon they came to
Sally Skittle's house and Noddy got out and went in at the gate - and,
dear me, on the path was an ENORMOUS puddle left by the rain!
Noddy stepped right into it. Splash!

"Oh - how wet my shoes are!" he said. "What will Sally Skittle say!"

Sally Skittle scolded him. "Dear dear! To think you didn't see a puddle as big as that!" she said. "And will you believe it, Billy Bear has done just the same! Take off your shoes, and I will dry them. Give me your gloves, too, and I will put them with your shoes."

So Noddy and Billy Bear didn't wear any shoes at the party, but they enjoyed it all the same. The floor was nice and slippery and the two of them slid up and down.

The tea was lovely and the cake was lovely too - the candles were made in the shape of skittles, and that made everyone laugh.

Sam Skittle liked the trumpet that Noddy brought him. Sally Skittle, his Mother, said that he liked it too much, because he wouldn't stop blowing it!

Noddy was sorry when it was time to go home. "I like the beginning of a party, and I like the middle, but I don't like the end," he said. "Why don't we have parties with only beginnings and middles, Sally Skittle?"

"Now, don't you begin asking me silly questions like Sam," said Sally. "Look, go and find your shoes, Noddy. There they are, over there, with your red gloves."

Billy Bear said he couldn't be bothered to put his on. "I'll tie my shoes round my neck and stuff my gloves into my pocket," he said.

Noddy put on the red shoes with blue laces. He didn't put on his gloves till he had shaken hands with Sally Skittle.

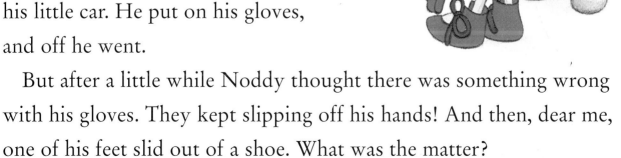

"Thank you very much for having me," he said. "I have had a lovely time."

Then out he went to his little car. He put on his gloves, and off he went.

But after a little while Noddy thought there was something wrong with his gloves. They kept slipping off his hands! And then, dear me, one of his feet slid out of a shoe. What was the matter?

Noddy stopped the car and got out. He put on the shoe again - but

his foot seemed much too small for it!
No wonder it slipped off - and, goodness
his hands were much too small for his
gloves, too!

"I'm going small!" suddenly wailed
Noddy. "Somebody's put a spell on me!
I'm going smaller and smaller, I know
I am! Soon I'll be so small that I won't
be seen - and then what shall I do?
I'll go and tell Big-Ears!"

So he got into his car again and drove at top speed to Big-Ears' little
toadstool house. He jumped out of his car and ran to Big-Ears' door,
one of his shoes falling off as he ran.

"Big-Ears! Big-Ears! Something dreadful is happening!" wailed Noddy, knocking at the door. "I'm going small. Ever so small. Look at my new gloves - they just won't keep on my hands - and look at my feet! My shoes won't stay on!"

"Good gracious! This is dreadful!" said Big-Ears in alarm. "But wait - your hat still fits your head! You can't be going small. Give me one of the shoes, Noddy."

Noddy gave him one, and after one look at it Big-Ears began to laugh and laugh. "Oh, Noddy! HOW silly you are! These are Billy Bear's shoes. Look, his name is inside - and his gloves, too! He has enormous feet and paws - so, of course, his gloves and shoes don't fit you!"

Dear me, Noddy was so very very glad! And see, off he goes to Mrs Tubby Bear's to get back his own shoes and gloves. He isn't going small after all!

BIG-EARS' UMBRELLA

Now once Big-Ears was very cross because it was raining and he wanted to go shopping and couldn't find his umbrella.

"I lent it to Noddy - and he didn't bring it back," thought Big-Ears. "Really, that's *very* naughty of him. Well, I must just take my old umbrella, though it's full of holes."

So he walked through the wood and down to Toy Village holding the old umbrella over his head. He did his shopping and soon filled his big square basket.

Then he set off home again. When he turned a corner he saw something rather peculiar in front of him. It was a very big umbrella over a very small person - whose legs were all that showed below the umbrella!

"Ha! That's my big new umbrella!" thought Big-Ears. "The one I lent Noddy. And those are his legs below it - I know his red shoes and blue laces! Now - where's he going with my umbrella, the little rascal!"

Well, Noddy was going to Big-Ears' house up in the wood! When he saw that it was raining that morning, he suddenly remembered that he hadn't taken back Big-Ears' umbrella.

"Oh dear - Big-Ears will want to go shopping today and he'll get SO wet!" thought Noddy. "And he'll be very, very cross with me for not taking it back before. He always says I should return borrowed things AT ONCE!"

So there he was, almost hidden by the big umbrella, on his way to Big-Ears' home. And there was Big-Ears behind him, laughing at Noddy's feet going in and out under the enormous umbrella.

"Little monkey - little scamp - only taking back my umbrella when it's pouring with rain!" thought Big-Ears. "Well - I'll make him carry my shopping for me all the way home!"

So what do you think he did?

On the top of the big umbrella was a large spike, sticking upwards - and Big-Ears very carefully placed his basket upon it! The spike held the basket firmly, and as Big-Ears had carefully covered up his shopping it wouldn't get wet!

"Dear me!" said Noddy to himself, "this umbrella suddenly feels VERY heavy! I wish it would stop raining - then I could put it down."

But the rain still poured down, and little Noddy staggered on, holding the umbrella over him, with the basket of shopping balanced on top, the spike holding it nice and firm.

Big-Ears walked behind, chuckling. He knew that the basket would feel very heavy, but it would certainly teach Noddy a lesson! On they went, up the path through the woods, and Noddy didn't even guess that Big-Ears was so close behind him!

"Hallo, little Noddy!" said Big-Ears, when they reached his house. "I see you've got my umbrella."

"Oh Big-Ears - you made me jump!" said Noddy. "Have you been shopping? Oh Big-Ears, I hope you didn't get wet. I've brought back your umbrella, and if I'd known you were shopping in the village I'd have carried your basket home for you too, to show you I was sorry I forgot about your umbrella."

"Well - never mind - you have carried it home!" said Big-Ears. "No - don't put the umbrella down - give it to me. There - look - my basket is on the umbrella spike - you carried it all the way!"

"Oh! No wonder I thought your umbrella was heavy!" cried Noddy. "Oh Big-Ears, you won't be cross about your umbrella now, will you - because I did carry your shopping all the way home!"

"No. I'm not cross," said Big-Ears. "But I shall be NEXT time you forget to bring back something you borrow."

"You won't - because I shan't forget, Big-Ears!" said Noddy. "I shan't - I really SHAN'T!"

BUMPITY BUMPITY BUMP!

"Hey, Noddy, hey! Take me to the market!" shouted a teddy bear who was standing at the corner of the street with a sack as Noddy came by in his little car.

Noddy stopped. "Hallo, Mr Bear," he said. "Get in. Put your sack at the back."

"What do you charge to go to the market?" asked the bear. Noddy didn't like him very much. He was rather dirty and his coat was torn.

"Sixpence," said Noddy, setting off. They hadn't gone very far before Noddy heard a little noise behind - bump - bumpity, bump.

"What's that?" he said.

"Oh, nothing," said the bear. "The road is so bumpy that the car makes quite a noise."

"All the same I'm sure I can hear something going bumpity-bump," said Noddy. "As if something was falling down from the car. I do hope it's not falling to bits."

"Of course not," said the bear. "Please don't stop, Noddy - I really must get to market quickly. I've some *beautiful* big apples in my sack, freshly picked this morning and I'm going to sell them for a lot of money."

Now the bear was telling a naughty story. He *hadn't* got apples in his bag! He only had potatoes, and not very good ones either! He also had something else in that sack - a big hole! He had cut one there himself, so that the potatoes would fall out one by one as Noddy took him along in his little car. What a peculiar thing to do!

They came to the market and then Mr Bear got out and went to collect his sack. He gave a loud yell.

"What's the matter?" said Noddy, anxiously.

"My apples! My BEAUTIFUL apples! There's not a single one left in the sack!" cried Mr. Bear. "Not one. They must have fallen out every time you went over a bump, Noddy. That's the worst of a silly car like this - it has such bad springs that not even apples in a sack are safe!"

"My car is a very good one!" said Noddy, fiercely. "I *heard* something falling into the road, but you wouldn't let me stop. I'm sorry about it, but it's NOT my fault!"

"It *is*," said Mr Bear, looking very fierce too. "Because of your silly bumpy car I've lost all my apples - and I would have sold them for twenty shillings."

"You would not," said Noddy.

"I would," said Mr Bear. "But as I don't expect you've got much money, I will only charge you ten shillings for losing them out of your car."

"Ten shillings! I've only got *two* shillings!" said Noddy. "And I'm not going to give you that. *You* owe me sixpence for taking you to the market!"

"We'll tell Mr Plod," said Mr Bear, and he beckoned to the policeman, who was standing in the market, directing traffic.

Mr Plod listened to Mr Bear's tale. "ALL my beautiful apples gone!" he wailed. "And all because of his bumpy car. I'm very kind only to charge him ten shillings."

"You must pay up, Noddy," said Mr Plod. "Pay the two shillings you have and..."

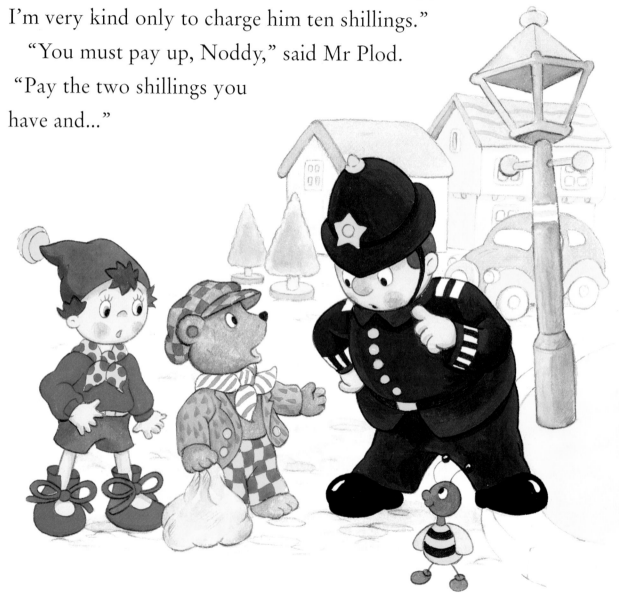

Just then Big-Ears rode up panting on his bicycle. He had a very big basket in front, because it was his shopping day. It was full to the brim with old potatoes.

"Hey, Noddy!" he called. "I've been trying to catch you up for ages. I was riding behind your car and I saw these potatoes falling out of a sack at the back. So I picked them up, put them in my basket - and here they are. You must have a big hole in that sack!"

"*Potatoes*!" cried Noddy. "But Mr Bear said they were his very best apples. Oooh, you fibber, Mr Bear!"

Mr Plod suddenly caught hold of Mr Bear.

"Ha!" he said. "This needs looking into! You've been tricking our little Noddy - you put old potatoes into a sack with a hole in it and said they were good apples. You're a bad bear. Now you just pay Noddy a whole shilling for his trouble, put your old potatoes into your sack and carry them away to the rubbish-heap!"

Mr Bear looked scared. He gave Noddy a shilling, and Big-Ears emptied the potatoes into the sack. Mr Bear put it on his back without a word and walked off with it.

Bumpity-bump! Bump-bump-bump!

Noddy gave a squeal of laughter. "Oh! He won't get far before his sack feels as light as can be! There go all his potatoes out of the hole, one by one!"

Bumpity-bump! It serves you right, Mr Bear. You shouldn't play horrid tricks on people.

"Big-Ears, thank you very much!" said little Noddy. "I've got a shilling instead of a sixpence! Let's go and spend it on ice-creams!"

So off they go together. Good old Big-Ears - he really is a help to little Noddy, isn't he?

NODDY AND THE FIRE-ENGINE

One afternoon, when Noddy was driving slowly through Toy
Village, he noticed a very peculiar thing.

A little house stood back from the road with a nice garden in front -
and out of one of the upstairs windows was coming a thin spiral of
smoke.

Noddy stared at it as he drove by. Why should smoke come out of a
window? Hadn't the house got any chimneys? Yes, it had four! Then
why did the smoke come out of a window?

"I wonder - I just *wonder* - if there's something on fire there!" said
Noddy, and he suddenly felt excited and his bell rang loudly on his hat.
"Perhaps I'd better knock at the door and ask if everything is all right."

So he drove back to the gate of the pretty little house. He got out of
his car and went up the garden path. He knocked loudly at the blue
front door and rang the bell. Rat-a-tat-tat! Jingle-jing!

Nobody came to the door, so Noddy went round the back. The kitchen door was locked and he couldn't make anyone hear - nor could he get in.

Then he saw a little note on the doorstep. "No bread today. Back tomorrow."

"Oh - the people have gone away!" said Noddy. "NOW what shall I do? I really must find out if something is on fire."

He went round to the front again, and saw that a tree grew

right up to the window out of which the smoke was drifting. "I'd better climb it," said Noddy. "It doesn't look a hard tree to climb."

So up he went and looked in at the window, which was shut except for a little crack at the top. Goodness - what a shock he had! A fire had been left burning in the room, and a piece of coal had jumped out on to the rug and was burning!

"Fire!" shouted Noddy, and almost fell out of the tree. "Fetch the fire-engine, quick! The rug's burning - and now the flame has reached a little table and one leg's burning! Fire!"

He tried to open the window a little more, to get in and throw the burning things out of the window - but he couldn't. Oh dear, oh dear -

the flames were now burning all the table, and a waste paper basket too - and soon they would reach the book-shelf and what a blaze there would be then!

"I must go to the fire-station and tell the firemen," thought Noddy. "Yes, that's what I must do."

So he slid down the tree and got into his car. Away he went, hooting madly to make everyone get out of his way quickly. Mr Plod saw him flash by and was very cross.

"Going along at sixty miles an hour!" said Mr. Plod. "I'll have something to say to you about this, Noddy."

Noddy arrived at the fire-station - but alas, the fire-engine wasn't there, nor were there any firemen to be seen.

"Where's everybody," yelled Noddy. "Fire, fire!"

A small beetle shouted back to Noddy. "They've taken the fire-engine to put out a fire on Farmer Straw's rick."

"Oh, goodness me!" said Noddy and raced his car up to the farm. Ah - there was the fire-engine standing quietly in the lane. The fire had been put out in the rick - but where were the firemen? Not one was to be seen!

"Fire! Fire!" shouted Noddy. The firemen were all down at the farm-house having some lemonade and cakes with the farmer and his wife. One put his head out of the door when he heard Noddy shout. He put it back again, laughing heartily.

"It's only little Noddy! He's seen our fire-engine and he's got all excited. He's shouting "Fire! Fire!" as if there really was one here!"

Noddy was very worried indeed. He couldn't *think* where the firemen had gone to. What was he to do?

"That dear little house will be all burnt down if I go to look for the firemen," he thought. "Oh - I wonder now - I do, do wonder - if *I* could drive that fire-engine!"

He slid out of his little car and ran to the gleaming fire-engine.

He climbed into the driving seat. Now - here was the steering-wheel - and there was the thing that started up the engine - and that must be the brake - he could only *just* reach it because his legs were so short.

R-r-r-r-r-r! He started up the engine - it moved off down the lane. Ooooooh! What a thrill for Noddy! His head nodded madly and his face went very red.

The fire-bell rang as he went along - and when he came into Toy Village everyone ran out to see the fire-engine, Mr Plod too. He stared with his mouth wide open at the surprising sight of *Noddy* driving the fire-engine!

"What next?" he said. "What next?" And he jumped on his bicycle and raced after Noddy.

Noddy came to the house where the fire was, and stopped the fire-engine. Dear me, there was a *great* deal of smoke coming out of the window now - and was that a flame?

Noddy leapt down and wondered how to get the hose and the water to the house. What did firemen do next? But he didn't have to wonder long because here came Mr Plod on his bicycle, red in the face with anger.

"What do you mean by this, little Noddy?" he roared - and then he suddenly saw all the thick smoke coming out of the window.

"See - it's on fire!" shouted Noddy. "I found the fire-engine but I couldn't see the firemen - so I brought the engine here myself, Mr Plod. How do we get the water to put out the fire?"

Well, Mr Plod knew all about things like that of course! A lot of people had come running up now, and he gave his orders quickly.

"You, Mr Straw, find the water under that iron grating there - take up the lid, that's right. And you, Mr Toy Dog, fasten the end of that hose to the tap down there.

"Turn on the water when I tell you! Hey, Mr Noah, help me to run the hose into the garden."

Noddy climbed the tree and looked in at the window. "Everything's burning!" he cried. "Bring the hose up here, Mr Plod. Shall I break the window?"

"Yes!" shouted Mr Plod, and CRASH, Noddy broke the window so that the hose could go through. He pulled up the hose himself, and then Tessie Bear climbed up beside him, and soon the water was pouring into the burning room, making a hissing, sizzling noise.

"Hurray!" shouted everyone. "Hurray! The fire will soon be out!"

"It's OUT!" shouted Noddy. "Nothing but smoke left."

"Come on down, Noddy," said Mr Plod, and Noddy climbed down, keeping as far away from Mr Plod as he could. But the policeman grabbed hold of him - and will you believe it, he set little Noddy on his shoulder and carried him all the way through Toy Village like that.

"Here comes Noddy, who saved a house from burning down!" he shouted. "Here comes Noddy, who drove the fire-engine all by himself - though he mustn't do it again unless he asks me. Here comes Noddy, so give him a cheer!"

And you should have heard the loud hurrays all the way down the street.

Big-Ears couldn't *think* what was going on when he came riding through on his bicycle.

When he saw Noddy being carried on Mr Plod's shoulder he was so astonished that he fell off his bicycle - bump!

"Noddy! What are you doing up there? Noddy, why are you so dirty, why is your face so black? Noddy why..."

You wait a little, Big-Ears, and hear Noddy answer your questions. You really WILL be surprised!

BOTHER YOU, MR JUMBO

Every day Mr Jumbo went to the station and caught the train. He was lazy and he liked to go to the station in Noddy's car.

"I don't like taking you, Mr Jumbo," Noddy said. "You're so heavy that you make the car go right down on your side, and you're so big that you squash me dreadfully. Please, I'd rather not take you."

But he had to, because whenever Noddy was in the ice-cream shop, which was next door to Mr Jumbo's house, Mr Jumbo came out of his front door and got into Noddy's car, which was parked outside.

Noddy kept finding him there, and then, of course, he had to drive him to the station.

One morning Noddy had done some shopping and he put his packet of butter on the seat beside him. Then he drove to the ice-cream shop and went inside. Out came Mr Jumbo, got into the car - and sat down heavily on the butter!

Noddy came running out. "Mr Jumbo! Did you move my butter? Oh, don't say you're sitting on it!"

Well, he was, of course - and when he got out at the station the butter looked exactly as if a big steam-roller had been over it and rolled it thin and flat. How upset Noddy was!

Now will you believe it, the very next day poor Noddy left six eggs in a bag on the seat of his car - and as soon as Mr Jumbo saw Noddy going into the ice-cream shop, out he came, got into the car - and sat down on the eggs!

When Noddy came out he saw yellow yolk dripping out of the side of the car, and he knew what had happened. Oh *dear*!

"Mr Jumbo! All my breakfast eggs were on that seat," said Noddy, almost crying. "Why don't you look on the seat before you get in? You're SILLY!"

"If you talk to me like that I'll bounce up and down," said Mr Jumbo loudly. Noddy didn't dare to say anything more.

There wouldn't be much left of his little car if Jumbo began to bounce up and down in it. He hoped he would pay him for the broken eggs, but he didn't.

For two days after that Noddy didn't go to the ice-cream shop, and Mr Jumbo had to walk to the station. It did him good because he was much too fat.

But the third day Noddy went to the ice-cream shop again. He simply *loved* ice-creams! He had just been to the toyshop and had bought three balloons, one for Big-Ears, one for Mrs Tubby, and one for himself. He had left them on the seat of his car, as usual.

Mr Jumbo rushed out of his front door. Aha! Now he could ride to the station again. He didn't look on the seat, of course. He just sat himself very heavily down on those balloons.

BANG! POP! BANG!

All the balloons burst under him with a tremendous bang.
Mr Jumbo had a terrible shock. He tried his hardest to get out of the
car, but he was stuck fast.

"Help! HELP, I say! Noddy! Your car is blowing up! It's exploding!
It went BANG, POP, BANG! I shall be blown up too. Help, help!"

Noddy had heard the bangs and the yells. At first he was scared -
then he guessed what had happened, and he grinned all over his little
wooden face. Aha! Old Jumbo had sat on his balloons, had he!

He ran out. "Help me out, help me out!" begged Jumbo. "Your car's
going to explode. It's gone BANG, POP, BANG already."

"You're stuck," said Noddy. "I told you not to get in any more.
I think I'll leave you there. If the car is going to explode it will serve
you right to be in it!"

"I'll pay you anything you like
if only you will help me out!" said Jumbo,
doing a little bounce.

"All right. Pay me a shilling for my
butter, and a shilling for the eggs
you sat on," said Noddy. "Quick -
before another BANG-POP comes!"

So Mr Jumbo paid up with a groan,
and then Noddy tugged and pulled,
and at last Mr Jumbo got out.

"Is my tail still on?" he asked
anxiously. Noddy looked.

"Yes. It hasn't been blown off.
But don't you get into my car
again, Mr Jumbo. It doesn't
like you!"

And off went Noddy to buy himself
some more balloons. Dear me, you
should have heard him laugh!

THE END

First published by HarperCollins Publishers Ltd as *Noddy Toyland Stories* 1997,
Noddy Bedtime Stories 1997, and *Noddy Christmas Storybook* 1997.

Noddy Toyland Stories, Noddy Bedtime Stories, Noddy Christmas Storybook
Copyright © 1997 Enid Blyton Company Ltd.

13 5 7 9 10 8 6 4 2

Enid Blyton's signature mark and the words 'NODDY' and 'TOYLAND' are
Registered Trade Marks of Enid Blyton Ltd.

ISBN 0-00-136115-5

Illustrations by County Studios

Printed and bound in Belgium by Proost